Cursed Touch

Broderick Coven #4

By AJ Renee

AJRenee

Cursed Touch

Copyright © 2020 AJ Renee

Edited by Angie Wade

Carter Broderick had been healing living beings for as long as he could recall. His gift had encouraged him to enter the medical field, and besides his family, it was his biggest love.

But everything in his life changed when *she* burst through the ER doors.

Vanessa Rayne was an ordinary woman. She made jewelry and was proud of her business but was pretty sure humans weren't the only residents of her city.

The supernatural world preferred to work outside of human knowledge, so word spread fast about the curious human.

With a target on his girl's back, can Carter protect Vanessa before she becomes another statistic?

also by aj renee

ST. FLEUR SERIES:

Widower's Aura

Always Mine

Duplicity

No Going Back

Taxed by Love

Complications

LOVE IN SCRUBS SERIES:

Joshua

Jason

Wes

BRODERICK COVEN SERIES:

Cursed Love

Cursed Sight

Cursed Whispers

Cursed Touch

Cursed Luck ~ *Coming 2021*

OTHER TITLES:

Finding Love at the Falls... (Short Story)

Fractured Fairytales Book One

Beauty Unmasked

Winter's Surprise

A Deadly World: Vampires in Paris

Billionaires Club

Unlucky in Love

Take Two: A Collection of Second Chance Stories

dedication

For all the first responders in our lives.

chapter 1

With her head bent forward and her keys in her hand, Vanessa Rayne's short brown hair fell forward as she flitted to the only blue key on the ring. She grabbed the key between her thumb and forefinger as she approached her second-floor apartment.

A small grunt sounded from nearby, and she rolled her eyes. Finn, her neighbor from the apartment beneath hers, must have left his window open again. She needed to remind him that no one wanted to hear him getting laid. He was a nice enough guy, but she was sick of hearing the grunts and moans of the men and women he slept with.

Vanessa slid the key into the lock as another grunt was followed by a closer hiss of pain. Her brows pinched together, and she peered over her shoulder to the stairs leading to her floor. Alarm filled her at the sight of her other neighbor, Tyler, climbing the final stairs to their landing. His face was pale, the muscles of his jaw clenched tight.

"Tyler?" Vanessa called as she removed her key from the still-locked door.

His head turned at the sound of his name, and a knot of worry filled her empty stomach. Tyler's normally bright-blue eyes were a dull gray, his lips were pulled into a thin line, and beads of sweat peppered his forehead. He gave her a dismissive wave and stumbled with his next step.

Vanessa shoved her keys into her jeans pocket and rushed to him. "Hey, what's wrong? What happened?" she asked, searching his face for clues. Her eyes moved down his body, rounding when they met his torn and bloody jeans. "Whoa!"

"Just a dog bite. I gotta go clean it," he said and hissed.

Vanessa shook her head. "Um, no. That looks awful, Tyler."

"Yeah? Well, it feels worse. Promise I'll be okay," he said and took another step in the direction of his apartment.

She put a hand to his chest before lowering to a knee for closer inspection. Staring at the jagged wound, she pulled out the small pack of tissues she had slid into her hoodie's pocket earlier that day. She carefully dabbed around the bite, and her eyes darted up and noted his pinched lips and shut eyes. The bite was inflamed, and his blood wasn't showing any signs of clotting. His jeans were soaking it up, but soon there would not be anywhere else for it to go.

"What kind of dog did this?" she asked, envisioning a monstrosity with elongated fangs.

Tyler mumbled unintelligibly, but she thought she heard him mentioning his herbs. Looking from his face to the bite, she knew there was no homeopathic remedy available to help the festering wound.

Vanessa pushed to her feet, then tucked herself under his arm to bear some of his weight. "Come on, let's get you to a doctor."

"No—"

"Arguing with me won't do you any good, so just save your energy and help me get you to the car," she said, cutting off his protest.

Her gaze shifted between Finn's door and the next step as she neared the bottom of the staircase. It was her luck that the one time she could use his strength, he was nowhere to be found. After what felt like forever, Vanessa managed Tyler down the stairs without breaking either of their necks. He floated in and out of consciousness, which only made the process scarier and harder.

She debated reaching into her back pocket and calling nine one one a few times, but if Tyler was like her, he wouldn't be able to pay the cost of an ambulance. By some miracle, she got him down from their floor and all the way to her car. She pulled the seatbelt across his chest, her heart pounding with the workout it received, and gave the injury one last glance before shutting the door and rounding her car.

Along the drive, she reached across and pressed two fingers to his throat, relieved to feel his faint pulse. She did not know what had attacked him, but she was pretty sure it was not a dog. Shifting her eyes from the road to his mouth, she noted there was no foamy saliva, but his lips looked rather dry.

"Do humans even get foaming mouths from rabies?" she muttered to herself as the hospital appeared in the distance.

Vanessa pulled her lower lip in and chewed. It was a nervous habit of hers when she faced a puzzle. As of lately, she did it daily. Things in town had become rather strange in the last year, but anytime she brought it up, no one else had noticed the same things.

One night she had peered out her window and saw a few rather large dogs strolling down the street on the sidewalk. Another time, she returned to her shop with new plants to replace her dead mums but found them as vibrant as the day she had planted them.

The list of strange happenings went on and left her with only one conclusion: magic was real.

Her eyes darted toward Tyler when he moaned in pain. "Maybe werewolves?"

Vanessa turned into the hospital and drove up to the emergency room doors. She set the car into park as movement drew her eye. Tyler's leg twitched and then his hips, torso, one arm, and the next.

Panic filled her at the unnatural jerky spasms wracking Tyler. Unsure what to do, she shut off the car and ran inside. "Help! Someone please help me!" she yelled into the lobby, alarming the people at the desk and a few sitting on hard chairs against the wall. A man standing at the side of the desk came rushing toward her before she even finished her cry for help.

"What's wrong?" he asked, his deep voice sending a tingle down her skin. His hand brushed her as he moved past, and an electric spark snapped her out of her panic.

Their eyes held for a strange moment before she raised a finger at her car, parked only twenty feet away. "Tyler."

The man nodded and ran out ahead of her. He wore black slacks that did everything to accentuate the round muscles of his ass and cover his long legs. Her body tingled once again, her nipples puckering with arousal.

"What the hell, Vanessa?" she muttered before joining him as he knelt beside Tyler.

He looked at the dog bite and the small pool of blood forming on her plastic floor mat. His jaw clenched at the sight. Pulling out a pen light, he examined Tyler's eyes before pressing two fingers against his neck. Vanessa watched with worry over her friend and intrigue over the stranger whom she assumed was a doctor. Before she could think further, he stood as a woman pushed a hospital bed out to them. Vanessa stepped back and watched them heave Tyler onto it.

He stabilized Tyler's leg, his fingers probing the skin around the wound. "What happened to him?" the doctor asked, his intelligent brown eyes captivating her.

Vanessa mentally shook herself, demanding she focus on Tyler and not the attractive man. "I don't know. He says a dog bit him, but that looks putrid. As I pulled up, his body began convulsing. He also lost consciousness on the way here."

"Are you family?" a woman in scrubs asked as Tyler disappeared with the mysterious doctor at his side.

Vanessa shook her head. "He's a friend." It was not entirely a lie, as she probably knew Tyler the best out of her neighbors. He was a nice guy, and they chatted briefly whenever they were outside at the same time.

The woman nodded. "Why don't you sit over here, and when we know more, someone will come get you?"

It was formed in a question, but Vanessa knew it was more of a statement. "Okay, but let me go move my car first."

Vanessa wiped the sweat off her brow as she returned to her car. She was suddenly wiped and ready for a nap. She slid into her car and released a heavy sigh. Whatever had bitten Tyler needed to be put down before it killed someone.

She rounded the hospital until she found a dumpster. After pulling up closely, she put the car in park and moved around to the passenger side. Carefully, as so not to touch the blood, she removed the mat and tossed it into the large green bin.

"At least he didn't get any on the carpet," she muttered and shut the door.

chapter 2

"Dr. Knowlen will have you all patched up in no time. It's a really good thing your girlfriend brought you in," Carter told the man, as he gripped the end of the bed, hoping he looked casual.

"Girlfriend?" Tyler asked, his brows pinched together.

An image of the short-haired brunette who had stolen the breath right from Carter's lungs came to mind. "The woman who brought you in?"

"Oh," Tyler said with understanding as he leaned forward to inspect the bite. His eyes narrowed before meeting Carter's with question.

Neither spoke, but Carter was sure the man suspected something had happened outside the scope of standard medicine. Before Tyler could ask, Carter gave him a curt nod and slipped out of the triage room. He could not risk anyone learning of his gift.

He hurried down the hall to the bathroom and locked himself inside. Leaning against the door, he shut his eyes as his head swam. Tyler had been on the verge of dying when he arrived. Carter had begun healing him outside, magic he could do in front of distracted patients, but once he'd gotten inside, he helped the man a little further along. It seemed it would take him an extra second to gather his energy after using so much magic.

The woman floated into his thoughts, and he recalled the way his body had vibrated at her nearness. It was the strangest reaction he'd ever experienced to a woman. When he cupped her shoulder to get her attention, the zing that had shot through his fingers surprised him. She lit his body on fire, stirring his dick like no one ever had.

"She's here with her boyfriend, you dimwit," he said and pushed off the wall.

Carter splashed cold water on his face and patted it dry with paper towels. "It's a good thing you're done for the day."

He was only at the hospital as a favor to a colleague who had asked him to consult on a particular patient. Carter's years of emergency care were behind him after specializing in pulmonology. At least, he'd thought they were, before he learned his family were witches and came from a long line of magic users.

Growing up, he had believed something was wrong with him. He even considered he was a superhero of sorts in his younger years. Whenever he'd gotten injured, he healed much faster than his peers. In time, he secretly mastered the art of healing others. It was what drew him to his profession.

He had managed to keep his gift a secret until last year, when everything turned upside down. His sister turned twenty-one, unleashing her bound powers and attracting the attention of things that went bump in the night.

He now walked around with the knowledge that werewolves, demons, witches, and God only knew what else actually existed. The world of magic contradicted his medical education, but so did his life-saving gift.

Carter checked in with the desk again before waving them good-bye. A quick scan of the lobby left him deflated when he did not see the woman. She was probably in the back by now, sitting with her boyfriend while he was treated.

Treated for a dog bite.

He thought on all his knowledge of dog bites and treating them, but nothing matched what he had seen today. A little voice in the back of his head warned him it was supernatural, but he refused to jump to that conclusion every time he heard of a strange case.

Sliding behind the steering wheel, he rolled his head back and forth and sighed. Carter had been healing people for as long as he could remember—both with medical advances and his magical ones. As he thought on the last year and the patients he knew for a fact were not human, his brows narrowed.

Facts were facts, and as he sat in his car with beads of sweat forming along his back, he realized one key fact. Human injuries, no matter how severe, did not tire or affect him, but injuries caused by magical beings sure did.

Carter pressed the brake and pushed the start button to his Audi A6. He backed up carefully, all the while analyzing the image of the bite and Tyler's symptoms. As he approached the streetlight that would take him home, he maneuvered the car into the left turn lane but then checked his rearview mirror and turned the wheel right.

There was still so much he needed to learn about their world. He knew if he went home, he would not be able to relax. Ryan, his brother-in-law, Serena, his future sister-in-law, and Peter, the Alumbra pack alpha, were the only experts he knew on these matters. Since Ryan was busy with Brandy and Gia, his daughter, and Carter had not spent much time with Peter, he pointed his car in the direction of Serena's shop, Sage Beginnings.

He'd driven past her shop a few times but had never gone inside. When he pulled open the door, a bell announced his arrival.

"Be with you in a second. Feel free to look around." Serena's voice floated from somewhere in the back.

Carter stood in front of the door and allowed his gaze to move over the tables and bookshelves filled with crystals, books, incense, herbs, and God only knew what else. The store itself had a distinct smell, one he could not put his finger on but instantly reminded him of his childhood.

He stepped between tables and moved to a bookshelf nearly overflowing with books. A book on wiccan healing caught his eye, so he reached for it.

"Carter?" Serena called, and he dropped his hand to his side.

Turning on his heel, he smiled. "Hi, Serena," he said and placed a kiss on her cheek.

"Hi," she said and cocked her head to the side. "What are you doing here—I mean, you've never come here before."

He raised a brow. "Sorry. Did I come at a bad time?" he asked and peered around the empty shop.

"No! I'm sorry, I'm just a little surprised is all." She waved toward the black curtain. "Come on, I'll make us some tea," she said and waved a finger in the air.

The sound of a lock reached his ears. "Did you just lock the door?"

"Mhmm…"

"Won't that be bad for business?" he wondered aloud as they moved through a back room with a few boxes of what he expected were more supplies.

Serena looked over her shoulder at him and chuckled. "And how many shops like mine have you seen around town?"

Carter thought on it and shook his head. "None?"

Her shoulder raised. "Technically there are two more, but they don't supply the things I do, and everyone knows I take care of them. If someone really needs something, they can call."

He followed her up the stairs at the back in silence, unaccustomed to conversation with Serena. She was perfect for his little brother, enough sass and intelligence to keep him on his toes—or off them.

Carter gave himself a mental shake not wanting to consider the latter. "Is this your old apartment?" he asked when he reached the top. A couch faced a large window to his right, and a doorway led to a kitchen to his left.

"It is," she called from the kitchen. "I've sublet the bedroom to one of my witches, and Ethan and I bought furniture to fit the new house."

His cheeks warmed. "Sorry I haven't been by to see it."

Serena chuckled. "You're allowed to have a life, Carter. Maybe then you, too, can get hit with the love bug."

His mind flitted to the woman earlier, and his heart, the traitor, sped at the thought. He slid a finger between his neck and button-down shirt. When the tea kettle on the stove whistled, he realized he'd become lost in his thoughts.

A moment later, Serena handed him a hot mug of tea. "Now, you want to tell me the real reason you came to see me?" she asked with a wave toward the couch.

Carter settled down, holding the mug between his hands as he gathered his thoughts. "Today a patient was admitted to the ER, and I happened to be there when his girlfriend brought him in. He was unconscious and, frankly, minutes from death."

Serena's brows pinched together, but she remained silent.

"She claimed he'd been bitten by a dog, but everything he experienced was... wrong?"

Serena nodded. "You don't think it was a dog?"

Carter shook his head and sighed. "The bite mark was larger than a normal dog, but it did seem to be the same. But, Serena, dog bites don't turn septic that quickly."

"You think it was a werewolf?"

He shook his head. "I don't know what it was. What I do know is when I heal human injuries, my recovery is minimal if at all, no matter the severity. Healing magical injuries hits me hard. Claudia knocked me out for a week. After healing the women we saved at the Sivella compound, I was out for nearly a week and a half, and that was after learning how to control it better."

"And how do you feel right now?"

Carter shut his eyes and took note of his body. "Right after? I felt weak and had to maintain composure as best as I could so no one would notice, but my head swam profusely. Now I feel like I could take a long nap, and even then, I'd still feel fatigued. Like I said, he was on death's doorstep. If I'd healed him all the way, I wouldn't have been in any condition to drive."

Serena nodded. "Drink your tea. It will restore your energy."

He looked down at the liquid and took a tentative sip. A bitter flavor burst on his tongue, followed by a nutty taste he could not identify.

"Carter, now that you're healing more often and have determined a difference with heals, you're going to have to take better care of yourself. I'll send you home with more of this maca tea. Its properties will help give you the energy you need."

"Thanks, Serena."

"As far as the bite? It sounds like a lycan bite. Once their saliva mixes with the tissues in our bodies, it's deadly. Your patient was really lucky you were there to heal him."

chapter 3

Vanessa stared into her cup of coffee, her eyes glazed as her mind wandered. By some miracle—or magic—Tyler had been released after a couple hours. He'd been prescribed amoxicillin for the infection and told to keep the wound clean.

He limped his way out of the hospital, but it was a vast improvement from the condition he was in when she'd brought him in. It just didn't make any sense to her.

Then there was the matter of the... doctor. She was not sure who he was, since the person who had discharged Tyler was a woman. But the man? Vanessa had dreamed of him all night. His brown eyes swallowing her in and her body vibrating with his touch... No man or woman had made her shiver like the one look from Dr. Tingles had.

Dr. Tingles was the nickname she had given him after a few hours of thinking about nothing but him and how he'd affected the nerves along her skin. His strong jaw, brown eyes, and dark hair that was a week past a haircut were all firmly planted in her mind.

She was nearly obsessing about this total stranger. There'd been something so familiar about him, a connection perhaps. Vanessa shook her head again.

"You sound like a lunatic," she chastised herself.

Then again, if magic really did exist like she believed it did, the chances of that man meaning something to her didn't sound crazy at all.

She looked at the time and realized if she wanted to check in on Tyler before going to her shop, she needed to get a move on. Vanessa chugged her now-lukewarm coffee before washing the mug and setting it to dry.

Looking down at her blouse, she was pleased to see she had managed to keep it stain-free. Red roses decorated the white fabric of her sleeveless top, and she'd paired it with dark-wash jeans and a pair of black wedges. Summer was around the corner, and she would enjoy every ray of sunshine they got.

Vanessa grabbed a hoodie and her keys and left the apartment. After locking up, she knocked three times on Tyler's door. She closed her eyes at the cool May breeze caressing her skin as she waited.

A minute later, the locked disengaged. "Hey," Tyler said.

Color had returned to his face, and it seemed he bore all his weight evenly. "Hey, I wanted to check up on you."

"Thanks, I'm feeling much better, thanks to you," he said.

She studied him closely, wishing she could see the wound on his lower thigh. "You look... better. Almost like nothing happened."

Tyler's eyes shifted as he chuckled. The sound was odd and made her wonder if he was nervous. "That's a good thing. I'd hate to look like death."

She bit her lower lip in thought. "See, that's exactly how you looked yesterday. Antibiotics are great, but they're not that great."

He shifted his feet. "Are you heading to your shop?"

She narrowed her eyes at his deflection. "I am..."

Tyler nodded. "Thanks again for checking up on me, but I'm good." His eyes darkened when they shifted toward a parking lot in the distance. "You should drive today."

Vanessa searched the lot for any signs as to why he would suggest she drive. A man was walking through it, and the breeze around them became a gust, causing her to blink rapidly. When she focused once more, the man was gone. "Uh, why do you say that?" she asked Tyler distractedly as she searched for the man. "Did you see the guy out there? One minute he was there, but the next he was gone?" she asked before Tyler could respond to her previous question.

Tyler cleared his throat. "N-no. There wasn't anyone that I could see. You saw a guy disappear?" He chuckled. "Maybe I should take you in today."

Her hard gaze landed on him. "I know what I saw. Look, feel better. I gotta go."

She drove to the shop that morning—not because Tyler had suggested it but because their little visit cut into her walk and she'd worn her wedges. There was no way she would hold up all day in wedges if she walked the mile to work, let alone the return mile home.

Vanessa didn't have the privilege of having any employees. Her small boutique made enough to pay the bills on the shop, rent on her apartment, her cell phone, and groceries for one, and she was able to set a little savings aside. The only reason she could afford as much as she did was because the landlady, Mrs. Ruby, kept the two-bedroom apartment that sat above it and gave Vanessa a killer deal on the place.

For some buildings in town, the second-floor apartments had separate entrances from the businesses below. It was nice because Vanessa was able to keep Mrs. Ruby's life separate from the boutique.

She pulled into the small lot in the back and parked next to Mrs. Ruby's Town Car. Vanessa smiled at the boat of a car as she passed it on her way inside. She flicked on the lights before checking all her tables were as she had left them. Satisfied everything looked great, she flipped the sign to open and unlocked the deadbolt.

Her gaze lowered to the planters in the front. Today they held marigolds, but her mind transported to almost a year ago when she found her dead mums had come fully back to life. Something in Helmond was different. She wished she could point and yell *a-ha* at the discovery, but would anyone listen to her crazy observation?

She went to the storage closet and pulled out the supplies for her latest project. There was no sense in wasting time or scaring off customers by creepily staring out the window.

Lost in the third intricate ring she had designed, twisting and manipulating the wire just right, she jumped when the shop's door opened.

"Welcome to Enchanted Ever After. If you have any questions, please let me know," she told the two women as they stepped inside.

One had a baby strapped to her chest in a black cloth, her hair pulled up high in a messy knot. The other nearly glided in a flowy skirt, her long auburn hair framing her face. They were both beautiful and held a mysterious energy her normal customers didn't have.

Vanessa lifted the velvet-lined drawer she had created to work on projects and slid it under the counter. She'd learned early on to keep her projects contained so she could help her clientele in a second.

"Thanks, honey, will do!" the brunette called back, a genuine smile tilting her lips.

The women wandered, showing each other varying items, when Vanessa remembered her latest addition. She grabbed two reusable bags with the store's logo stamped on the side and moved toward the pair. "I forgot. Here, for your shopping needs. Just put whatever you want to buy in there and bring it to me to ring up."

The women nodded and smiled with a quick thanks. As Vanessa's hand neared their skin, it warmed. Part of her instincts warned her the women were dangerous, and another part wanted to lean in closer to the energy around them.

"You okay?" the redhead asked.

Vanessa cleared her throat. "Hmm?"

"You look a bit pale," the brunette said.

Vanessa twisted her wrist. "Oh, shoot, is it really one o'clock?"

They offered her a kind smile. "Yeah, lose track of time?"

She nodded. "Yeah. If you need anything, please let me know."

Vanessa smiled, but as she returned to the back, her brows pinched at the strange sensation she got from them. Surely her observation was due to lack of food. Moving to the storage closet, she peered back and noticed the women turn away from her. Inside, she knelt at the small fridge she kept with snacks and grabbed the plate of grapes, ham, and cheese. She shoved a few pieces into her mouth, and her eyes rolled back as she chewed.

"How'd you find this place again?" the redhead asked the brunette, and Vanessa paused near the storage door.

"That *time* at Peter's. Remember when I needed air? Well, I was walking and noticed these dead mums," she said before lowering her voice. "Let's just say I tested earth that day."

Vanessa's face scrunched at the words. She wondered what *testing earth* meant, but before she could think more on it, she swayed. Leaning forward, the plate knocked against the door. Her face flamed as she stood straight and sucked in a breath.

"Are you okay back there?" the brunette called.

Vanessa walked out with an embarrassed smile decorating her face. "Yeah, sorry. I skipped lunch and went to grab something, and I just got a bit dizzy. Did you find anything you like? If there is a piece that catches your eye but something on it doesn't fit, I can customize it."

"Wait... These are all *your* designs?" the redhead asked.

Vanessa put her food under the counter, and her gaze shifted from one woman to the other as she nodded. "Yeah, there are a couple pieces in the display over there that aren't, but the rest of the jewelry is."

Their eyes rounded. "You're really talented. Have you ever worked with crystals or natural gemstones?" the redhead asked.

"Wait, before you answer, please take a few bites of food. We really don't want to scrape you off the floor after fainting," the brunette said.

The redhead laughed. "New mom," she said, by way of explanation.

Vanessa inwardly cheered. "Would you like some?" she asked, offering the plate.

"We just ate lunch around the corner. Now eat."

Vanessa popped a few pieces of ham and the Colby Jack cheese in her mouth and hoped she didn't look like some feral animal as she chewed before her customers.

"I'm Brandy, by the way," the brunette said, her eyes cast downward on the cherub tucked away, "and this is Serena."

Vanessa gave them a little wave and covered her mouth with a hand. "Vanessa."

"Nice to meet you," they said and waved a hand toward the food, telling her to have another bite.

Once Vanessa got enough to hold her stomach over, she tucked the plate away and dabbed at her mouth with a napkin. "I'm so sorry about that, but thank you. That should help my sugar levels."

"Are you diabetic?"

She shook her head. "No, but when I don't eat, it plummets and makes me sick and even nauseous." Vanessa moved around the counter and toward a display in the corner. "Is this what you were looking for?"

Serena moved forward, and her fingers caressed a few of the pendants pinned to the velvet. "Wow, these are beautiful."

"Thanks."

She stepped to the side so they could shop comfortably, but Serena placed a hand on her shoulder. "Wait," she said, and heat flooded Vanessa's skin.

Her eyes narrowed on the slim hand pressing against her as she disappeared into her thoughts. The heat wasn't sexual. While Vanessa found both women attractive, it wasn't the same. An image of Dr. Tingles popped in her mind, and her heart stuttered to life. Whatever energy surrounded these women was unlike anything she had ever experienced.

"Serena," Brandy hissed.

"Oh, I'm sorry, I didn't mean to—"

Vanessa studied them closely. "No, it's okay. You just... startled me..."

"I'd like them all, and I was wondering if you could make some of those chakra bracelets with lava stones?" Serena asked carefully.

Vanessa's eyes rounded with surprise, but she managed to bite her tongue. "Yeah. Sure. Great! I have a shipment of the stones coming in, so let me know how many you'd like, and we can create the order. It won't take more than a day or two once it's in."

"I want one hundred," Serena said, her brow quirked up.

"Oh... Well, then I'll need about a week, two max. If I may ask," she said as she pulled out an order form, hoping it wasn't covered in dust. "Why so many?"

Serena smirked. "A few will be gifts, but I own Sage Beginnings, and my customers would love these."

Vanessa recognized the store's name but had never gone inside. She did not know what Serena sold for a living, but she just helped Vanessa pay the rent.

chapter 4

Carter dropped into a seat, careful not to jar the plate of food in his hands. Varying conversations flowed around him, and he marveled that Gia, his baby niece, was sound asleep among his family's everyday chaos.

"You okay?" Claudia asked. She was engaged to his brother Max, who was slightly younger than Carter.

Carter forced a smile and nodded. "Yeah, just tired."

It wasn't entirely a lie. He had been getting shit sleep for the last week, ever since he saw the woman in the emergency department. She was never far from his mind, and it was beginning to piss him the fuck off. He could not do anything about the woman because she had a man.

"You don't seem fine, but I do understand having things going on in your mind. If you want to talk, I'm here," she told him and took a bite of her food before her daughter, Katia, ran up to her.

"Momma! Look what Auntie *Se-ena* got me!" Katia announced excitedly.

Carter's gaze moved from Katia's joyful expression to the small swing moving Gia back and forth. Her soft baby face remained angelic, even with her cousin's excited chatter. Even if Carter was the type to intervene—and he wasn't—he could not chide the child for being so exuberant.

Claudia and Katia had been through hell, and their happiness meant the world to not only his brother but his whole family. They had come a long way in the last few months. It made him wonder how the other women, the ones he had healed in the compound, were doing.

Beaten, raped, and held hostage for God only knows how long, the women were all in extensive therapy, including Claudia. One day at a time was all they could focus on, and he hoped that under the watchful care of Peter's pack, they could flourish as Claudia had.

As one of seven, Carter was used to loud environments. He loved the sound of his family, and after his father's passing, he and his siblings had continued their tradition of family dinners. Only, he found them harder to attend as his siblings found their mates. He was thrilled they had found love and were sickeningly devoted to their mates. But it did not mean he needed to be reminded about it for hours on end.

He would eat his dinner and spend some time with them and then he would get the hell out of there. He planned to enjoy a whiskey while his thoughts trailed to the mysterious woman when he got home. He was not going to kid himself. He knew none of it was healthy. His dreams and thoughts were not becoming less frequent as time passed. If anything, they were becoming stronger.

"Seriously, this shop is so freaking cute. We need to take you guys there!" Brandy told Debra and Andrea. "But, Serena, did you notice something was, I don't know, *off* about Vanessa? Vanessa is the woman who owns the shop."

"You mean when I touched her shoulder and she kinda wigged out?" Serena asked.

"Yes! If I didn't know better, I'd say she felt the magic swirling around us. Have any other humans noticed it?" Brandy asked.

Ethan perched on the side of the couch next to Carter, with a plate of food in his hands. "Why are they talking about the woman you've been thinking about the entire time you've been here?"

The food on Carter's fork fell onto his plate, and his eyes darted toward his little brother's. "What'd you say?"

Ethan held up a hand and stood. "Sorry, I know I promised I wouldn't pop into your head without invitation, but you've been over here moping, and I was worried, and—"

"Shut up, E, and repeat what you said!" Carter snapped, the room quieting at his words.

Ethan looked around, his brows pinching in worry. "The shop owner they've been yapping about... She's the same woman I saw flash in your mind."

"Ethan," Junior and Edward growled.

"We told you to stay out of our fucking heads," Edward snapped.

"Language!" Brandy, Andrea, and Debra called in sync.

Ethan raised his hands, careful not to spill the contents of his plate. "I know, I know! But look at him!" he said and waved his hands toward Carter. "I've never seen him like this, and it worried me, so I just wanted a quick peek and well…"

"Who's the woman?" Claudia asked softly.

Carter peered around the room. Everyone's attention was on him, including Katia, who had quit playing with her new bracelet to watch the adults yell. He sighed and shrugged. "I don't know who she is. I was leaving Schwab Memorial and as I said good-bye to the ladies working the emergency department desk, she came running in, calling for help."

"What was wrong with her?" James asked as he neared the others.

Carter shook his head. "Nothing. She was fine, but her boyfriend was in really bad shape. They claimed it was a dog bite, but he was minutes from dying…"

"The lycan bite?" Serena asked, and he nodded.

"What lycan bite?" Ryan asked.

"He came to me for help, and we determined the bite must have been a lycan's," Serena said. "But you never mentioned the woman..." She left the statement hanging, no accusation but curiosity filling her tone.

No longer hungry, Carter pushed to his feet and dumped his plate and its contents into the trash. "No, I didn't. The woman brought in her boyfriend with a lycan bite, and I healed him enough so the doctor on duty could finish treatment. There was nothing else to say." He turned toward Ethan, his lips thin and his jaw hard. "I would appreciate it if next time you stayed out of my thoughts and allowed me to keep my private thoughts private."

"I get it, but are you seriously telling me you didn't want to know that the shop owner they've been gabbing about is the same mysterious woman who has been on your mind all night?" Ethan asked, no apology in his words.

Carter threw up his hands. "What part of *she has a man* do you not understand, Ethan!" he yelled. Unable to take more of the conversation, he slid through the crowd and hightailed it home.

He tossed his keys and cell phone onto the kitchen island, not bothering to watch them slide across the smooth surface as he moved to his handmade cherrywood bar. He grabbed the bottle of whiskey with one hand and a glass with the other, poured two fingers of amber liquid, and swallowed it in one gulp.

"Shit!" he said into the silence before pouring another two fingers.

With the bottle capped and back in its spot, he carried his whiskey to the couch and turned on the TV.

He didn't care what was on. Carter just needed noise to drown out the mess his life had become nearly overnight. Crossing his ankles on the large ottoman before him, he leaned back against the plush couch.

Not only could he not get the woman out of his head, now his entire family knew about it. "Thanks, E!" he said with another shake of his head before bringing the glass back to his lips. The smooth liquid warmed his insides as it slid down his throat.

He wondered what the chances were that he had met her the same week his sisters had stepped foot into her store for the first time. There were so many questions he wished he would have asked before storming out of the family gathering, but he just could not stay. He sucked in a deep breath at the pressure on his chest.

If he was not a doctor, he would have been driving himself to the hospital. Then again, as a doctor he knew better than to drink his worries away. Sucking in a breath through his nose, he shut his eyes and willed the stress to depart his body. He was anxious and wound so damn tight, he doubted he would get much, if any, sleep that night. Good thing he was not on shift the next day.

Why did the first woman to intrigue him past a good lay have to be taken?

It wasn't her looks. He had seen plenty of beautiful women. This one... Vanessa, he thought they had called her... "Shit, even her fucking name is beautiful." *This* woman was different... was special. He couldn't help but wonder if she was his.

He wondered how Brandy, Ethan, and Max had known who theirs were. Junior and James were not technically with their soul mates, implying theirs had passed, but their women were perfect for them, and Edward did not bother speaking of such things.

The spark when he touched the frantic woman had dug deep within him and refused to release him of its sting. Why did she affect him so strongly? Was she a witch, a werewolf, or something entirely different?

chapter 5

The large order Serena had placed left Vanessa in the best mood. Even days later, she woke with a smile on her face and a bounce to her step. Sure, the sexy dreams with Dr. Tingles she'd been having may have had something to do with her state in the mornings. Then again, her vibrator was getting a lot of TLC since the trip to the ER.

Tyler had completely healed, and she had a sneaking suspicion that if she peeked at the wound, there would be no signs of it. It was something she would add to the list of strange goings-on in her town. She saw him one other time after checking in on him, and if she did not know better, she would say he was trying to avoid her.

At least her Good Samaritan behavior had brought her tasty dreams. Too bad her mind would not let her stay there, in dreamland. Before she could think further on it, her cell phone vibrated violently against the glass counter. The name on the screen caused her face to split into a grin as she accepted the call.

"Hi!" she said excitedly. "Please tell me you're back!"

Georgia chuckled. "Missed me that much?"

"Yes! How was it? You have to tell me everything," she demanded, leaning back into the chair.

"Dinner tonight? I really could use a juicy steak," Georgia stated, and Vanessa imagined her best friend drooling at the thought.

"I'll close now if you want an early dinner," Vanessa said, pushing to her feet.

The phone rustled before Georgia spoke. "No, no. I'll meet you there at closing. I need to shower off my stink and do a tick check."

"Ew..."

Georgia laughed. "Part of camping, Nessie."

Vanessa rolled her eyes at the nickname but didn't object. Georgia had been calling her Nessie ever since she'd met her in fourth grade. "See you at seven then, but we'll have to order an appetizer because there's no way I'll make it until the entrees."

Georgia laughed. "Eat a damn snack, woman. See you later."

Before Vanessa could say good-bye, the call ended. She beamed with excitement at the prospect of seeing Georgia. It had been a few weeks since her friend had decided to go backpacking, and while she did it often, it did not stop Vanessa from missing her.

Vanessa liked the outdoors, but Georgia's love of all things nature ran deep. She even went on to become a park ranger. As the years passed, they went in different directions but maintained the same tight-knit bond they always had. She could not wait to tell her all about Dr. Tingles.

***

"If your mother is more conservative, this one will be the better choice," Vanessa told her customer. The woman thanked her as another customer stepped inside. She had been swamped for the last two hours, something she could thank Serena for. It seemed her customers had indeed loved what she had to offer and decided to come by and see for themselves what else Vanessa made.

"If you have…" Her words trailed off, then she squealed with delight at the sight of Georgia in her shop. "You're really here!" she said and rushed to embrace her.

Georgia chuckled. "Missed you too, girl."

When they parted, Vanessa noted the customer watching their reunion. "Sorry, this is my best friend, Georgia, and she's been playing out in the woods for like three weeks."

The woman laughed. "Welcome back to civilization."

"Thanks," Georgia replied before following Vanessa to the counter. "Shop looks great! I like the extra displays you added."

"Thanks, I came up with a few more items, and well…" Vanessa shrugged and gave her a knowing smile. "Go take a look for yourself."

As Georgia meandered through the shop, the customer brought Vanessa the earrings and necklace set she had been eyeing for her mother. Vanessa did her best not to hurry the woman along, but she was all that was between them and dinner. She walked her to the door and turned the sign to closed.

Within fifteen minutes, Vanessa closed out and they were hurrying to the steak house two blocks over.

"You did not eat a snack, did you?" Georgia asked as they almost jogged down the sidewalk.

"Girl, I was swamped before I could even think to grab a bite."

"Nice!"

The hostess took them to their table right away, thanks to Georgia's brilliant idea of calling ahead. A teen came by almost immediately with a basket of rolls and butter before slipping away.

Vanessa dove into the basket and bit off a chunk of bread. Her eyes shut with ecstasy as soon as the warm bread touched her tongue. When someone cleared their throat, her eyes popped open and caught Georgia's amused expression.

Georgia leaned forward. "I'm glad to see nothing's changed, but if you're not careful, you're going to make some of these men pop wood, and last I checked, this is a family establishment."

Vanessa giggled at her friend's words and the serious tone she used to deliver them. "Sorry, I'm just seriously starving."

"I told you to get a snack…"

"Like I said, I tried but got so busy I wasn't able to sneak away for a bite," she said around a mouthful of bread.

Georgia took pity on her and shared some of her trip, and Vanessa spoiled her dinner with bread. They put in their orders, and by the time the food arrived, her stomach was settled. It had been too long since they shared a meal, but it would only become harder when they found their someone and settled.

Vanessa pushed her plate forward, too full to finish the steak and roasted potatoes. Looking around the restaurant, she spotted a couple smiling as their fingers interlaced on the tablecloth. Blushing at their show of intimacy, her gaze landed on a man who placed a nearly raw piece of steak in his mouth.

She gasped when his eyes flashed yellow gold in the dim light, before his now-dark orbs met hers.

"What?" Georgia asked, her brows knitting as she searched the restaurant.

Vanessa shook her head. "I-I don't know… I swear that man's eyes flashed red."

Her friend sat straighter and paused when she met the man's gaze. For a moment, she thought she heard a guttural vibration emanate from Georgia, but before she could analyze it, the sound ended.

"He looks normal to me. Maybe what you saw was blood oozing from his steak."

Vanessa peeked at the table but found both the man and his companion were gone. "Weird," she muttered.

"What?" Georgia asked.

"He's gone... They're gone," she said, noticing both plates were nearly clean of food.

"Good riddance. Now, tell me what else has gone on since I saw you last. Have you learned for yourself what Finn has to offer?" she asked of Vanessa's neighbor as she waggled her brows suggestively.

Vanessa choked on her sip of wine. "Eww... I'm not sure I want to catch whatever he's offering."

"Don't you want to release some of that tension?"

"Don't you have the same problem?" Vanessa replied.

Georgia sighed. "I do, and I sure as hell wish I could find the right guy to help me with it."

A woman walking past their table gasped, her hand flying to her mouth as her cheeks reddened.

Vanessa mouthed her apology and gave her friend a look of warning. "Well, I guess we're both in the same boat... Wait, what about the guy from your gym? Patrick, Paul, Pacey—"

Georgia chuckled. "Peter?"

"Yeah, him. I thought you were all hot for him."

"Oh, he's hot all right, but nah, he's not right for me." Georgia sat back in her chair and took a deep pull of her wine. "So you haven't met anyone new? What about Tyler on your floor?"

Vanessa leaned forward with wide eyes. "Oh my God, I can't believe I forgot to tell you!" She caught her friend up on finding Tyler injured and meeting the sexy-as-sin Dr. Tingles. Her body warmed, and her thighs clenched tightly as desire pooled between them at the memory.

Georgia pushed her water toward Vanessa. "Take a drink, Nessie. You're all sorts of flushed just talking about this man."

She chugged, but the ice water did nothing to soothe the fire burning in her belly. "I don't know what it was about him, Georgia. I've never reacted so strongly to a man."

"And you have no idea what his name is? Do you think Tyler might know?"

She shook her head. "No idea, and well, Tyler got pretty cagey about his bite. I swear I thought he was going to die in my car and then hours later, I was driving him home." Vanessa bit her lip in thought. "I guess it's another strange event. It's like aliens have swooped in, and we have a case of pod people."

Georgia shifted in her seat, and her eyes shifted around them. "You can't seriously still believe that."

Hurt clouded her eyes. "You don't believe me…"

Georgia leaned forward. "I believe you, honey. Let's say you are right. What if the wrong person hears you and... I don't know. I don't want anything bad happening to you. That's all."

chapter 6

"I'm here for a gift," he told himself for the hundredth time. Carter stood before Enchanted Ever After's large windows, peeking into the "boutique," as his sister had referred to it. Most pedestrians passing him on the street probably assumed he was window-shopping, checking out the display of trinkets meant to entice passersby.

He wasn't.

His heart raced, his pulse thumping against the skin at his neck. He licked his suddenly dry lips and swallowed thickly. Running a hand over his face, he exhaled and then sucked in a deep breath.

"Quit being a coward!" he chided and stepped toward the door. His slick palm pulled the handle, and he stepped inside.

Soft music flowed throughout the shop, and he breathed in a flowery scent. The space was inviting and peaceful.

"I'll be right there!" a woman said from out of sight.

He wondered if it was *her*. A couple weeks had passed since he saw her at the hospital. The clear memory of a spark he had experienced at their touch remained at the forefront of his mind, but her face and smell had blurred over time.

Carter forced his feet toward a random display so he would not look like an idiot gawking around the store. His hands shook with each step, and his body hummed with an unseen pulse of energy.

Before him was a case of earrings. He tried to remember if Andrea's ears were pierced and mentally kicked himself in the ass for not knowing. She had been a part of their family for years, and he did not know her favorite restaurant, let alone if she wore earrings.

He pulled out his phone, opened his messages, and clicked on Brandy's name. He sent her a text and sighed as he moved to a display with bracelets.

"Please let me know if you—" Her eyes widened, and her lips parted as their gaze met. Her throat worked as she swallowed hard, and his ears began to ring at the sight of his mysterious woman. "If you need *anything*..."

His mind went to dirty, sexy images of her fulfilling his needs. Her pink tongue darted out across her lower lip, and a sweet blush crept up her neck and to her cheeks. He needed to say something, rather than continue standing there like some dolt.

Sucking in a breath, he relieved the pain forming in his chest from holding his breath at the sight of her. "Hi..." He nearly winced at himself for his inadequate greeting. "You're the woman who brought her boyfriend in with the bite." He mentally patted himself on the back for sounding like the intelligent man he was.

"You're Doctor T... the doctor who helped him." Her voice was shaky, and Carter could not help but deflate when she did not correct him.

A pang shot to his heart, and he regretted coming to see her. It would only freshen the feeling she was someone to him. If she was taken, he would not be that man. There were not enough sparks in the world to allow himself to do such a thing.

Taking what wasn't yours was what had caused the women in his family to be cursed—before Brandy and Ryan had been able to end it.

Refusing to look like a dick by running out, he stared, unseeing, at the jewelry in the case in front of him. He really could use a gift for Andrea that was not another gift card.

"Are you shopping for yourself or someone else?" she asked, taking another step in his direction.

The damn invisible thread between them urged him to close the distance. "Someone else," he said, and he could have sworn he saw a flash of something cross her face. Could she feel jealousy toward a woman who did not exist?

Boyfriend, he reminded himself before he looked too far into her expression.

"My sister-in-law's birthday is coming up, and I'd like to buy her something," he said.

"Oh." Her single word was breathy, then a smile that did things to him brightened her face. "Do you know what she likes?"

On cue, his phone vibrated against his thigh.

Brandy: She has two holes in each. Why?

"She wears earrings." He shrugged as he slid the phone back into his pocket.

The woman laughed, and the sound was sweet as it flowed over him. He wanted to hear it again. "You have a pretty laugh," he said before he could stop himself.

Her cheeks became a deeper rose color at his compliment, and his chest puffed with pride. "Thanks." She moved past him, and her scent wafted to his nose. She smelled sweet and flowery. "Here are some earrings. I'm guessing you don't know if she likes dangly ones or studs?"

His brows rose.

The woman chuckled, and his dick stirred in his pants. "Favorite color? Animal? Hobby?" she asked.

"She and my brother like to flip houses," he stated as he realized how little he knew of the woman his brother loved.

The woman shook her head, and her smile was teasing. "Okay, well do any of these look like something she might wear?"

Carter forced his eyes toward the display. It was a hard feat with the beauty standing next to him. "Um...

maybe those," he said, pointing at a charm with a stack of books. "She likes to read."

"Okay, that's good. Why don't we set these aside. I have a few things that appeal to the bookworms in our lives." Earrings in hand, she returned to the counter, her hips swaying in a mesmerizing pattern, causing him to lick his lips. "I have a matching bracelet for those earrings. They came out really good and have been a hit."

He followed her to another case as his words pushed past his desire-induced fog. "Did you make these?" he asked in wonder.

A timid smile tipped her lips. "A lot of things in the store are my creation, but I have some I've bought."

"Wow," he said sincerely. "You're really good."

She paused and met his eyes. "Thank you. I guess we're both good with our hands."

"Excuse me?" he asked as his brain short-circuited with images of the many things they could do with their hands.

"Well, doctors use their hands quite a bit when handling patients," she said, and he was thankful she had missed the underlying innuendo of her words.

"Oh, yes. Add the bracelet to the earrings," he told her after one quick glance at her craftsmanship.

She nodded, but instead of adding it to the earrings, she leaned past him. "I promise I'm not trying to sell you the entire store, but this is a book sleeve. You can put the book you're currently reading or your tablet in it for safe keeping, instead of shoving it into a purse where it can be damaged. Not to say you have a purse, but readers who are female and have purses..."

Carter grinned at her flustered words. "Nope, I don't have a purse, and I have no one's purse to hold." She bit her lower lip, and he was tempted to pull it free but managed to restrain himself.

She cleared her throat. "That shelf down there also has cups, mugs, wine glasses, and bookmarks for book lovers. Go ahead and take a look, and I'll set this down with the earrings," she said, waving the bracelet back and forth.

Turning his back toward her, he grinned at the knowledge he made her nervous. It was another reminder that what he felt was not one-sided.

"How long have you owned this shop?" he called as he knelt for a closer look of the items she'd mentioned.

"About three and a half years now, but I've been creating things since high school. My skill has vastly improved since then," she said, and he earned another sexy chuckle.

Taking in her words, he realized he was older. "A lot of ambition for someone so young," he muttered as he rose with a ribbon bookmark in his hand. When he faced her, he met her hard eyes. "I didn't mean that—"

One well-groomed eyebrow rose as she crossed her arms under her breasts. The action drew his attention to them, but he knew better than to allow his gaze to drop. "Well, what did you mean?"

He'd pissed her off. While he felt bad for it, a bigger part of him enjoyed the vixen hiding behind her professional façade. Carter strode toward her. "I didn't mean to insult you. I'm impressed by your talent. My father taught me at a young age to never bring up a woman's age. If he were around to witness my grave error, he'd have socked me good, so please accept my apology."

chapter 7

Vanessa's chin, which had tipped up in defiance, dropped at the sight of the grief reflecting in his eyes. "How long?"

"How long what?" he asked, his face scrunching in confusion.

An invisible energy urged her to step forward, but she fought it. Any closer and their bodies would touch, which she craved, but in order to keep her head on straight, she could not allow it to happen. "How long has your father been gone?"

His gaze darted to the side as he shoved a hand through his hair, his fingers digging in and messing it up. "Oh, just over a year now."

Before she could stop herself, her arms wrapped around his waist and a cheek pressed to his chest. "I'm sorry…" He smelled woodsy and masculine, a delicious combination that caused her stomach to flutter.

After a moment of hesitation, he returned the embrace and rested his cheek on the top of her head. She was not sure how long they stood like that, but she did not want it to stop. Vanessa fit perfectly in his arms. His firm body aligned against her softer one. A calm washed over her at the innocent embrace. She belonged there.

At the realization of where her thoughts had gone, she sucked in a breath, memorizing his enticing scent, and pulled back. His pupils were dilated, his jaw muscles clenched tight.

Vanessa bit the corner of her lower lip. "I'm sorry. I shouldn't have—"

He shook his head. "I should be the one to apologize. I don't want to cause you and your boyfriend any problems."

"Huh?" she muttered, her nose scrunching with confusion. "Boyfriend?"

Dr. Tingles cocked his head to the side. "The man from the hospital?"

Her eyes widened, and she shook her head vehemently. "Oh, no… Tyler's *not* my boyfriend."

"He's not?"

"No. He's my neighbor."

"Your neighbor?" he asked.

Their conversation seemed to drop fifty IQ points as neither of them could articulate a complete thought. "Yeah, Tyler's my neighbor. I came home and found him trying to climb the stairs to our floor, and yeah, no. Not my boyfriend. I don't have a boyfriend."

She studied her shoes at her overuse of the word boyfriend. Time stood still as she realized he had falsely assumed she dated Tyler. *Did he care if she was seeing someone?* she wondered, thankful her lips did not vocalize the question.

His hand moved to her neck, and a zing of something dark and delicious licked through her. His thumb put pressure below her jaw, forcing their gazes to meet. He studied her as his palm pressed against her racing heartbeat, and goose bumps covered her flesh.

Slowly, he lowered his face until his lips brushed hers, and her mind melted on contact. She grabbed onto his wrist for balance at the feather-soft kiss. Vanessa should have been outraged he had taken her being single as an open invitation to be kissed, but she couldn't drum up the emotion.

She *wanted* to be kissed by him, the man she dreamed of both day and night.

The G-rated kiss lit her body on fire, its heat warming her to the core. A tender brush of lips should have never affected her so strongly. Lips did not have the power to reach into your soul, yet it was exactly what was happening between them.

He pulled back, his eyes shut and his nostrils flaring with frustration. "I should have asked first, but I needed to know…"

"Know what?" she whispered, trying not to cover her lips with her fingers.

His eyes met hers, a dark brown with flecks of amber hidden within. "If I was imagining this pull to you."

Her lips separated as she sucked in a shuddering breath. "I feel it too."

The door opened, and they jumped apart like teenagers caught in the throes of passion.

"I'm sorry. Did I interrupt something?" Georgia asked, her nose scrunching before she took in Dr. Tingles and her eyes widened.

He looked from Vanessa to Georgia with a question on his lips, but he shook his head. "I'll take these things, please."

Vanessa nodded and skirted around the counter. A flush covered her entire body as butterflies performed acrobatics in her stomach. Georgia kept her distance, but Vanessa could feel her friend's watchful gaze on them.

Dr. Tingles placed a hand over hers as she wrapped the items in tissue paper. "Have dinner with me," he whispered.

She knew absolutely nothing about this man. No, that wasn't true. She knew he could be tender with his kisses, he was a doctor of some sort, and he was sexy as hell. Some unseen force was insisting she tell him yes.

"I don't even know your name," she said in lieu of what she really wanted to say: hell yes.

"Carter Broderick."

"Vanessa Rayne."

He smiled and his eyes crinkled, softening the serious lines of his face. His smile faded, and he turned to look at Georgia over his shoulder. Her friend did not bother to pretend she was not staring at him.

"Do you two know each other?" Vanessa blurted.

"No."

"Kinda."

"Carter Broderick," he said, offering Georgia a hand.

Georgia studied it a moment before moving closer to accept it. "Georgia Reed."

Another silent moment passed while the two of them studied each other until Vanessa could take no more. "What's going on?"

Georgia released Carter's hand and stepped around the counter to stand hip-to-hip with Vanessa. "Nothing. How do you two know each other?"

"We met a couple weeks ago," Carter said.

"He's the doctor who helped Tyler out," Vanessa said, giving Georgia a warning look.

"*He's* Doctor T—oof." Georgia grunted when Vanessa's elbow connected with her side.

Carter cocked his head, his eyes dancing as they met Vanessa's. "Been talking about me?"

Her face became enflamed at the slip-up. "Just told her a nice doctor helped Tyler out."

"Uh-huh," he muttered, clearly not believing her half-truth.

She squinted as she studied them both. "Now, how do you two know each other? Kinda isn't an answer."

Georgia shook her head. "We've never personally met. I have met his sister, Brandy. She's close to Peter."

"How do you know it's *his* sister who's dating Peter?" Vanessa asked, trying to follow along.

Carter chuckled. "They're best friends, not dating. Brandy just got married."

Vanessa swiped the credit card he'd set on the counter as she let the information bounce around her head. Their town was not small by any means, but what were the chances of her best friend and the man her body literally vibrated for were in similar circles? It was not glowing-red-eyes odd but strange nonetheless.

Carter slipped his card back into his wallet as she turned the screen toward him. No one spoke as he went through the prompts. "Phone number?"

"That's just in case you want to join the VIP club, where I'll text no more than twice a month," she said to assure him.

Carter shook his head. "No, I'd like *your* phone number."

Her heart stuttered under her breastbone as she ignored a low growl from beside her. "Why?"

He smirked. "Seeing as you didn't answer my last question, I can call you and ask again."

She pursed her lips in thought, ignoring the voice in her head screaming yes. "If you're talking about dinner, you didn't actually ask me out."

He smiled. "Vanessa, will you please have dinner with me?"

She studied him as butterflies flew around her stomach.

"Oh, for goodness' sake, just tell him yes," Georgia muttered before glaring at him. "If you hurt her in any way, I promise my bite is worse than my bark."

He chuckled at Georgia but didn't respond, his attention directed at Vanessa. "Well, what do you say? Will you go out to dinner with me, tonight?"

Vanessa nodded, a stupid grin lifting her lips as she put out a hand. "Give me your phone." Carter unlocked the device and handed it over. "There, you have my number, and I have yours," she said after sending herself a text message.

"Be ready by six and text me your address," he said as he grabbed his bag and phone.

"Tell me where, and I'll meet you there. I don't give out my address on first dates," she told him seriously.

"Fair enough. Georgia, it was a pleasure meeting you," he said before turning on his heels and heading for the door.

Georgia grunted in reply, but neither of them spoke as he walked away. Holding the door open, he gave her a panty-melting smile over his shoulder, and her thighs quivered in reply.

Carter Broderick was unlike any other man she had met.

chapter 8

Carter: Luca's Trattoria on 8th. Looking forward to seeing you...

He hit send and ignored the rapid beat of his heart. It had not slowed since he'd stood in front of her boutique. Vanessa... Even her name soothed the numbness he lived with.

It took everything in him to not deepen their kiss. He was eager to learn more about her and better understand how she knew Georgia.

Thanks to the last year, he had learned plenty about his supernatural world. No doubt about it, Georgia was a werewolf and part of Peter's pack. Carter had briefly considered reaching out to the alpha to learn more about her, but he refused to give her the satisfaction. She was clearly protective over Vanessa, and he was admittedly pleased to know she had someone in her life who could keep her safe.

It was evident to him Vanessa knew nothing about her friend's true nature—something she was better off not knowing. The more he learned about the real things that went bump in the night, the less he wanted to find his mate.

And like the jokester that fate seemed to be, he found Vanessa just when he had settled on never searching for her. He had seen both the pretty and ugly side of soul mates. The bond between his sister and Ryan and his brothers, Max and Ethan, with their mates was mind-boggling to say the least. But in all three scenarios, they had gone up against some gnarly situations.

Unlike the others, Vanessa did not show any signs of being anything but human. Maybe their path would involve less violence and anguish.

Carter's only power was of healing. Max and Ethan each had two powers, and Brandy seemed to have them all. James could see the dead, and Junior's power of suggestion aided him in both his career and personal life. Edward was the biggest mystery, as luck was always on his side, but no one knew too much of their private brother.

If something came up against Vanessa, Carter would have to enlist the help of his family and Peter to protect her—something he was loathed to admit, even to himself.

Vanessa: See you in an hour.

Her text drew him back from his musings. She was not a woman to ramble in her texts, nor had she been upset that he'd taken a couple of hours to tell her where.

Carter set the bag with Andrea's gift on his island and the bouquet of wildflowers he'd picked up for Vanessa next to it. Opening one cupboard after another, he realized he did not own a vase. He grabbed the large plastic cup he'd acquired at the movie theater and filled it with water before setting the flowers inside.

He emptied his pockets on the island and hurried to his bedroom. He removed his clothes, tossed them into the basket in the corner of his bathroom, and turned the knob to his walk-in shower to hot. A few minutes later, the water cascaded down his body as he peered around the large open space with multiple shower heads.

His mind wandered to Vanessa, and he wondered if she would approve. Cream-colored tiles, which Brandy had helped him pick out, covered the walls and floor. A long bench seat lined part of one wall, and he envisioned the feel of the cool tile against his body as Vanessa straddled his hips.

Shower sex had always been cumbersome and something he'd avoided until he remodeled his home. He had yet been able to test out the space, but his dick was eager to take Vanessa for a ride.

With his dick hard from his errant thoughts, he turned the knob to the right and hissed at the cooler water. He brought forth memories of the putrid smells he'd experienced as a doctor and breathed easier without his erection clamoring for attention.

Carter dried off quickly and did not bother with the towel when he moved to his closet. Living alone had the benefits of nudity whenever and wherever he chose. In the closet, he grabbed a burgundy button-down shirt and a pair of black slacks.

He decided to forego the tie entirely and rolled the sleeves to his forearms. With a quick glance at the time, he ignored his clammy skin and strode to his kitchen where he slipped his wallet and keys into his pockets.

"Calm down, it's not the first time you've gone on a date," he chided himself.

His phone chimed from the charger where he'd set it and he prayed it wasn't Vanessa canceling on him.

Brandy: Come over. We're ordering pizza.

Carter: Thanks, but I have plans.

Brandy: Plans?

He shook his head at his nosy sister's surprise.

Brandy: Oh! You went to the shop to see Vanessa?

His lips formed a thin line before he leaned against the counter and exhaled. Switching text windows, he drew up Ethan's number.

Carter: Seriously?

Ethan: Hey, don't look at me. I stayed out of your head. Serena went by to pick up an order, and I guess your girl mentioned it.

His girl.

Brandy: Serena and Ethan are here too, as you now know. Well, if you change your mind, bring her on by with you.

Carter chuckled dryly. There was no way in hell he would bring Vanessa by his sister's on their first date. He wanted her all to himself.

He did not bother replying to either of them and grabbed the rest of his things and the flowers. If he left, then he could arrive before Vanessa to ensure they had a private table for two.

Inside the restaurant, he sat with his back to the wall, his leg bouncing under the table as his eyes remained trained on the entrance. Vanessa was set to arrive at any moment, and he was nervous as hell.

Carter wiped his palms down his pants and took in a deep breath. He could not remember the last time his nerves had gotten the best of him. He took another pull from his water, and movement caught his attention as he set the glass down.

Vanessa.

She stood still as she searched the tables for him. A black dress fit her body like a glove, reaching a few inches above her knees and dipping low enough to tease him with cleavage. She was absolutely stunning with her hair framing her face.

His dick stood to immediate attention, and he was thankful she had not spotted him quite yet. He adjusted himself carefully and stood, hoping she would not notice the bulge pressing against his zipper.

Vanessa's gaze landed on his, and she rolled her red lips. He moved to her chair and grabbed the flowers he'd set down earlier. Surprise registered on her face before her lips tipped up with happiness.

"Hi," she whispered when she reached him.

He kissed her cheek and inhaled the sweet scent emanating from her. "You're gorgeous," he told her and allowed himself to take all her in.

Her cheeks reddened. "Thanks, you look pretty hot yourself."

Carter grinned and handed her the flowers. "I hope you're hungry," he said and helped her into her seat.

"Starved. I'm always hungry to be honest," she admitted, her gaze cast downward as she fiddled with the bouquet on her lap.

Carter pulled a nearby chair to them. "Here, put those on here so you can be more comfortable. Last I checked, a woman with a healthy appetite was always a pro in my book," he said and winked.

"It's all fun and games until I get hangry," she told him so seriously he chuckled.

"Well, we should put our order in quickly to prevent that," he told her as the waiter approached them. He ordered a pinot noir after they discussed their choices. Once he decided on lasagna, he set the menu down and stared. Everything about her drew him to her: the line of her neck, the slope of her full breasts, the flare of her hips, and even the cute way she chewed on her lip when she seemed nervous or in deep thought.

"You're staring," she muttered without looking up.

"I can't help it, but I apologize if it makes you feel uncomfortable," he said and raised his glass of water to his lips, wishing it were a bit stronger. "I think I've eaten everything off the menu except for the vegetarian platter. I'm sure you'll love anything you decide on."

She nodded and set the menu down. "I was deciding between the lasagna or the *frutti di mare*. There's no way I could pick the vegetarian platter. I need meat in my life."

The sentence hung between them, but he managed to swallow the chuckle threatening to burst free.

Her chest flushed a rosy red, and she shook her head. "You know what I meant!"

Carter raised his hands in defense. "I didn't say a thing, sweetheart."

Vanessa sipped from her water, and he watched her throat move with the action. A sudden image of her lips wrapped around him flashed in his mind before he shook it away.

"So, I've been wondering..."

"About what?" he asked, and the waiter returned, halting their conversation.

With their wine poured and their orders put in, they each reached for the stem of their wine glasses. *"Salute!"* Carter said, tipping his glass toward her.

"Salute."

The smooth, fragrant wine exploded on his tongue before sliding down his throat. "Mmm... That's good. Now, what have you been wondering?" he asked and leaned forward after setting his glass on the table.

Vanessa swirled the wine a few times before setting it down. "Very good. Well... How did you find me?"

"Would you believe me if I told you it was fate?"

chapter 9

She tipped her head, confusion written across her face. "Fate?"

"I know it sounds crazy," he said and laid his hand atop hers. A current of need sparked at his innocent touch. "I'm sure it sounds like another line from another man, but deep down... I know you know it's true.

She looked from their hands to her lap as she chewed on her lip, effectively removing the lipstick she had applied for the occasion. "It's nuts," she muttered.

Rather than be insulted, Carter chuckled, and the sound flowed over her skin, sending tingles straight to her core. "It's mental, and that's coming from a professional," he teased, bringing a lightness to the seriousness. "Look, I've been with and met plenty of women. Unfortunately, my profession seems to draw out the crazy, but I've never felt this." He paused as he sat back, breaking their physical connection. "This... I don't know what to call it. I feel alive around you, like my cells are losing their shit, bouncing around in excitement. After meeting you, I couldn't stop thinking about you."

Her heart raced in her chest, thumping loudly against her breastbone in an attempt to break free. His words both exhilarated her and scared the living shit out of her. Not because she thought he was crazy... No, rather because she understood exactly what he was trying to say without coming across as some psycho.

"This is our first date," she whispered.

He leaned forward once more and reached for the hand she'd brought closer to her body. "Shit, I'm screwing this up entirely. I sound like a stalker who belongs in an institution. I'm sorry, Vanessa. You're right. This is our first date. I shouldn't have—"

"I feel it too," she blurted and turned her palm up.

He froze, and the slight trembles she expected came from his leg stopped.

She sucked in a breath and decided that if he could be raw with his honesty, she could too. "I couldn't stop thinking about you either. When I'm around you, I feel something. I can't describe it, but I know I've never felt it before."

He squeezed her hand. "One more thing because I want to lay it all out." He waited for her to nod and continued. "I'd been at our weekly family dinner, lost in my head thinking about you, when I overheard my sister and sister-in-law talking about some shop they'd gone to. I don't know why, but in my gut, I knew the shop owner they mentioned was you. I'd hemmed and hawed for quite a bit before stepping inside your boutique today."

Her brows pinched before her eyes widened with understanding. "Brandy and Serena?" she asked.

The smile that lit his face spoke of the love he felt for the women. "Brandy is my baby sister, and Serena is engaged to my brother Ethan."

"Wow... what a small world," she muttered, but before she could say more their food was delivered to their table.

They each took a few bites after releasing the other's hand. The delicious food excited her taste buds as her mind tried to wrap around the information bomb. Vanessa was prone to being led by her mind and not her heart, so while the two warred often, she found them coming to some sort of consensus on the current situation. With Carter a few feet from her, her body hummed, eager to be the one to take the lead for once.

"Tell me about your family?" he asked after a few minutes of silent eating.

Vanessa swallowed her bite as she stabbed her fork into the seafood. "Normal middle-class family. My parents are still happily married, and I was an only kid after they had trouble conceiving any more."

His fork clattered on the plate. "I can't imagine not having my siblings. Did you like being an only kid?"

She shrugged and took a sip of the wine as it soothed her erratic nerves being around him. "I don't know any better. I've at least had Georgia most of my life, so I guess she's like my sister from another mother."

He nodded. "She seemed..."

"Mean?" she asked, a brow lifted and a smirk threatening to burst free.

He shook his head. "Nah, protective. Although, I imagine her bite would leave quite the mark," he joked.

"How about you? Any best friends who'll try to protect you?" she asked before taking another bite.

He grinned. "Yeah, five brothers and a sister. We've all been protective over each other. Other than them—and now their significant others—I haven't had a close friend since probably medical school. As a doctor, my time has been rather occupied."

She nodded. "Will you have time to date?" she asked and held her breath. Connection or not, she needed to know if this thing between them would lead her to a heartbreak like no other.

Carter met her eyes. "For you, I'll make time. I've just never had anyone come in my life who's made me want more. I occasionally meet up with some buddies, but to be honest, it's not like the friendship you have with Georgia."

Vanessa wiped the corners of her mouth. "Georgia's great. I don't know what my life would have been like without her."

A commotion at the front of the restaurant drew their attention before the smell of wet, moldy dirt reached them. A woman cracked her neck and stared down the hostess. "I want a steak. Why can't I get a steak?"

"I'm sorry, but you're upsetting our customers, so you need to go," a man stated as he joined their small gathering.

"Come on, Nikki, we can get something down the street," another woman, equally as disheveled, told the first.

Nikki's eyes glowed for the barest second, causing Vanessa to blink her eyes rapidly as she gasped.

The woman whispered something to Nikki, and she nodded.

"I won't forget this shit!" The glare Nikki shot the group before turning on their heels sent chills down Vanessa's spine.

"You okay?" Carter asked, pulling her attention back to him.

"Did you see that?" she asked, her brows pinched tight.

He shook his head. "It's awful being an addict. I hope they find the support they need."

"Huh?"

"Isn't that what you meant? That was quite the scene."

It was Vanessa's turn to shake her head. "No, I meant did you see her eyes glow yellow?"

A shadow crossed over his face as he moved his head ever so slightly from side to side. "Yellow?"

"Yes, yellow. Something is going on in this town, I swear." She muttered the latter to herself. "Red eyes, glowing eyes, plants that come back from the dead, large-ass dogs..." She shuddered as the memories returned.

Vanessa chewed on her thumbnail as she considered the scene. "Alcohol? Can it cause hallucinations?" she asked before waving him away. "No, never mind. I wasn't drinking when I saw the large dogs or when the mums returned."

"Vanessa?" Carter asked firmly as he stood beside her. His gaze drifted to the tables around them as he smiled awkwardly. "Ready to head out?"

The billfold was closed on the edge of the table, and she realized she never noticed him pay the tab. The stares she was receiving from the tables nearby were a clear indication she had spoken the words out loud and most certainly not in a whisper.

Vanessa smiled apologetically at the customers and took Carter's offered hand. He threaded their fingers and guided them through the tables until they stepped into the fresh night air. Carter released her hand, and she could not believe she had messed up their date so quickly.

Before her heart could deflate, his arm wrapped around her shoulders and drew her into his side. Neither spoke for minutes as he guided them down the sidewalk. They passed other couples, friends, and the occasional family out for a stroll.

They entered Alumbra park, trees lining the sidewalk until the canopy opened above them. Carter picked a bench toward the center and held her hand. His thumb drew lazy circles on her hand, and little sparks danced across her skin.

"I'm sorry, I don't normally sound like a lunatic," she murmured, unable to meet his gaze.

Carter squeezed her hand. "That scene was pretty unsettling, but no, I don't think you're a lunatic."

"At the risk of driving you away... You're sure you didn't see her eyes glow yellow?"

Carter took in a deep breath before shaking his head and looking at the stars barely visible above them. "No."

An alarm went off in her mind, alerting her of his lie. She pulled her hand into her lap as tears brimmed behind her lids. "I can tolerate a lot of human sin, but I won't stand to be lied to."

chapter 10

Carter felt like the scum of the earth.

A few things had become clear to him over the past few hours. One, logical or not, Vanessa was his. Two, even as a human, she was not blind to the supernatural around her. And three, he was the biggest fool for thinking he could lie to her.

His mouth opened and closed a few times, briefly wondering if it was how fish felt when they were pulled out of water. When Vanessa pushed to her feet without a word or cursory glance, it took him exactly 0.5 seconds to get up and take hold of her.

She could not leave. Not after he'd found her.

"Wait!" he said as he searched for the right words. Words that would not hurt her further. Words that would help keep her safe and ignorant to the other world.

She pulled free but turned toward him. Her arms wrapped around her middle, and pain reflected in her eyes as her stubborn chin raised to him.

Carter shoved a hand through his hair again, and he was sure he managed to rip a few strands out at the roughness. "I'm a doctor, Vanessa. If someone heard me talking about seeing glowing eyes, I…"

He did not know what else to say. Leaning on his profession was the coward's way out but not entirely untrue.

She shook her head. "While that may be true, I refuse to date a liar. Thank you for dinner."

He watched her walk away, a sharp pain bursting through him at the sight. Everything in him screamed to follow her, but if there was any chance of fixing the mess he made, he needed to let her go for now and figure it out.

***

Carter dragged himself to work and disappeared into his schedule. The monotony of helping others did not soothe the ache of finding and then losing his soulmate, but it made the seconds go by.

His front door shook at the banging it received, pushing him to sit up on the couch. Running a hand down his face, he sighed before opening the door. "I'm surprised it took you this long," he told Georgia over his shoulder and returned to the living room. Giving the werewolf his back was probably the second stupidest thing he had done in the last month, but he could not drum up the energy to care.

"What the hell did you do to her?" Georgia snapped before the door slammed shut.

Carter peered past her, nodding with surprise that the door was still attached to its hinges before returning to the couch. "What did she tell you?" he asked, not bothering to deny he was at fault as he laid his head back. The couch dipped but she remained silent. Carter rolled his head toward her and raised a brow.

"She's not right," Georgia said.

"And you assume because she's not right I did something wrong?"

Her nose crinkled. "You look like shit."

"Thanks, I feel like it too."

"Fucking witches... What the hell happened?"

Narrowing his eyes, he asked, "Does she know the truth about you?"

Georgia's eyes rounded. "Hell no. It would put her in a lot of danger, especially since she's human."

He nodded. "Did you know she believes 'something is going on in this town'?" he asked, curling his fingers with air quotes for added measure.

"What do you mean?"

Carter recalled what had happened on their date night. "On the one hand, she thinks she's losing it, but on the other, she knows what she's seen."

"And why is she upset now? Did you embarrass her, or does she think you're nuts for agreeing?" Georgia asked.

He shook his head. "Like you, I want to protect her... so I lied, and she saw right through it."

"Oh no..." Georgia said and dropped her head back on the couch, shutting her eyes.

He sighed. "How do I fix this?"

"Why does this matter to you so much? You could move on and find yourself a witch and add more pains in the asses to this world."

He scoffed. "I'm glad you think so highly of me when you don't know shit about me or my family." A shadow crossed her face, and he turned to face her. "What? What aren't you telling me?"

"If your sister kept to herself, my brother would be alive."

The words hung in the air as Carter sorted through the past year. "That's a bold statement to make, wolf... My sister hasn't killed any werewolves from the Alumbra pack. If anything, she's saved them."

He shook with anger, his magic flowing through him at an alarming rate.

Georgia pushed to her feet and paced the tiled floor in front of his large TV. "If Ryan kept his distance, she wouldn't have been pulled in, and Peter wouldn't have become enamored with her. Because of his stupidity, he pulled us into battle at the Sivella compound, and my brother was killed."

He forced his mind to process her words before he shook his head. "You weren't there at the compound."

Her glowing yellow eyes met his as her body vibrated. Carter wondered if she would turn, and not for the first time, he wished he had offensive magic. Healing power would not do shit if she went all wolf on him.

"Maybe if I'd been there, he'd still be alive!"

He remembered the name of the wolf they'd lost as he scooted to the edge of the couch. "Reni didn't die because of my family, Georgia," he told her, using the same tone he did to deliver bad news to patients. "Your brother was a warrior... a hero. Would you really rather have left all those women in that madman's hands?"

"Yes! If it meant having him back, yes!"

Carter pushed to his feet and shook his head. Taking a measured risk, he moved toward her and wrapped his arms around her. Georgia struggled, but something told him it was more from grief. She could have shoved him away with a pinky if she really wanted to.

"No... You don't mean that. It hurts like hell to lose someone you love. Reni died so those poor women could live. He knew the mission was dangerous, but he went there for them. That could have just as easily been you. You'd never wish that on someone," he told her, one hand running over the back of her head and the other keeping her steady against his body. "I was there and wish I'd never seen it, but I'm glad I was there to heal their physical injuries. The invisible scars those women bear run deeper than any shit you or I could imagine. Reni helped us save them, and you should be proud of him."

Carter held her until her sobs were no more and the fight within her disappeared. He kissed the top of her head without a word and moved to the kitchen. "The bathroom is down the hall if you'd like a moment while I pour us a drink."

A moment passed before he heard her soft footfall and the door click. Carter leaned against the counter and stared at his ceiling, pushing back the images that still haunted him. Even after Reni's heart quit beating, Carter had tried to revive the wolf. He would never share that with Georgia, but he meant what he'd said.

It seemed their supernatural community was linked more than he knew. Carter did not realize it because he didn't spend much time with the Alumbra pack, not nearly as much as his sister did. He shook his head as he recalled Georgia's description of Peter being enamored with Brandy. The alpha held a deep love for her, but since they were without a mate bond, their connection was of brother and sister. Peter would not learn from Carter that Georgia, and quite possibly others, blamed his affection for the loss of one of their own.

Georgia had not witnessed the pain on the alpha's face when Xander, his beta, had notified him of Reni's death. Carter knew she was grieving, and he hoped his words helped.

The bathroom opened, drawing him from his thoughts. He grabbed two of the old-fashioned whiskey glasses Brandy had gifted him when he graduated medical school and crossed the kitchen and living room.

Georgia took the glass and nodded. He watched her over the rim as she sipped, pleased to see her savoring the liquor. The smooth liquid slid down his throat and warmed his insides. He moved to the large glass sliding door and stared into his darkened backyard.

"You asked why I didn't move on... why I didn't find a witch." He paused and faced her, leveling her with a stern expression. "Vanessa is my soul mate."

"You mean symbolically?"

"No."

"How? You just fucking met her!"

He shook his head. "You of all people know we don't get a choice in our mates, Georgia."

Georgia tipped back the rest of her drink before dropping to the couch. "But she's a fucking human."

Carter shrugged. "And she's still mine. She's mine, and she doesn't fucking want to see me again because I lied to her. I made her feel a fool and then she caught me in the damn lie, a lie that was meant to keep her safe."

"Fuck!" she said and dug her fingers into the hair at her temples.

Carter scrubbed his face and took another sip. "You have to help me. I can't lose her, and I don't know how to undo this mess without making it worse."

chapter 11

She could not stop thinking about Carter. His lying, sexy-as-sin, and intelligent ass would not leave her waking or sleeping mind. Over a week had passed since their first—and only—date went down the shit hole.

Vanessa attended her customers, maybe with less exuberance than normal. Georgia had not been around much to help her relieve her mind, and Vanessa had exhausted every comfortable position of her couch and bed for reading.

Looking for a change of scenery, she grabbed her laptop and tablet and walked to her favorite coffee shop. Beating the Saturday rush of students meeting up for study sessions, she found a corner table after ordering a black coffee and chocolate croissant.

It was not the healthiest of choices, but at this point, she just wanted to find her happy place. With her coffee in hand a few minutes later, she settled down to read. The shop was waking up as more customers arrived for their shots of joe, and she disappeared into her latest book.

After forty-five minutes, she was annoyed and rubbing her temples. Reading a love story may have not been the best idea with the heartache she carried around. She thought she felt a connection with the man, and the disappointment at learning she was possibly wrong hurt more than his lies.

Taking a break from the story line, she slid her laptop from its bag. She logged in and checked a few of her open orders before pulling up a web browser. Between Carter's lie and all the things she had noticed, she decided to investigate it further.

Vanessa searched for any accounts of people with changing eyes. One news article a few years back had mentioned it and a medical doctor provided his insight:

Without treating the individual in question, I can't tell you the reason their eyes appeared yellow or red. However, I can attest these cases are oftentimes the result of rare conditions. Jaundice, for example, may make eyes appear yellow, while some cases of albinism may cause eyes to look red or pink due to lighting conditions, making the blood vessels more visible.

"Ugh," she groaned and pushed the laptop away.

"What's the matter, little duckie?" a man dressed in dark-wash jeans and a white T-shirt asked.

Her fight-or-flight response kicked in, his presence warning her of imminent danger. When he leaned in closer, his gaze narrowed on her search. His lip raised, and she swore he snarled before setting his dark eyes on her.

"Tsk tsk—"

"Hey! Get the hell out of my shop!" a woman snapped from his other side. "You know better," she warned, a veiled threat dripping from her three words.

A shadow crossed his face before his gaze roamed down Vanessa's body. She had the distinct feeling he was memorizing her for some unknown reason. Goose bumps broke out across her skin, and she shivered with unease as he stood to his full height. A low growl emanated from his chest when he looked at the woman before hurrying from the coffee shop.

"Vanessa?"

She turned to the sound of her name and realized it had not been the first time it was said. "Brandy?"

"Are you okay? He didn't hurt you, did he?" Brandy asked.

She rubbed her arms, hoping to create some heat in her numb limbs. "No, just creeped me out."

Brandy stepped closer before kneeling at her side. Her gaze slid to the open laptop and narrowed. Vanessa reached out and slammed the lid down, unable to take another unrequested opinion over the matter.

"What brings you here on a Saturday?" Vanessa asked.

Brandy's lips pinched and twisted a moment as she studied her. She pushed to her feet and shrugged a shoulder. "I'm the manager here. I've been working a few hours a day since having Gia so the place doesn't get overrun with scum."

"Do you get them often?" Vanessa asked.

"Huh?"

"Scum. Do they come here a lot? I don't get people like him in my shop."

Brandy shook her head. "No, I don't suspect you would get many testosterone-filled jerks in your boutique." She chuckled. "Here, let me get you some tea so you can come down from that excitement."

Vanessa could not help but feel Brandy giving her side glances, even after the woman's attempt to brush off the situation. That asshole had most definitely planned to comment further, after expressing his disapproval over her search, until Brandy kicked him out—not that Vanessa was upset he had been urged along. He had unsettled her to the core.

Brandy rounded the counter with a cup of steaming hot tea and set it on the table away from Vanessa's electronics. "Here you go. It's really hot, so give it a second."

"Thanks, you really didn't have to do that."

"It's the least I can do for Carter's woman," she said with a wink.

Vanessa's heart stuttered, loving the sound of *Carter's woman* before remembering it was not her. "I'm not Carter's woman," she said, a slice of pain causing her to suck in a breath.

Brandy tipped her head to the side before she pulled a nearby chair next to her. "I don't understand. What happened?"

She shook her head. "I'm not really sure I should be having this conversation with you. You're his sister."

"That I am, and if he did something, I'm going to whoop his ass like I wasn't his baby sister."

Vanessa could not stop a chuckle from slipping free. "It's nothing, really," she fibbed, ignoring her inner voice, which scolded her for the lie. Lying the same way he had.

"Errr," Brandy said, mimicking the sound of a game show buzzer. "It's something. Out with it."

Vanessa looked around the busy coffee shop, but no one seemed interested in the two of them. She dropped her gaze to her lap, where her hands twisted with nerves. Sucking in a breath and needing someone to talk about it, she decided to take a chance and spilled it all.

Brandy's face took on a variety of emotions, ranging from confusion to surprise to deep in thought. But she never looked at Vanessa like she'd lost her marbles. "So you're saying you've noticed all of this, mentioned it to Carter, and he called you a liar?"

"No! He denied seeing the person's eyes change at the restaurant, but he lied."

She nodded slowly. "I—"

"Brandy!" someone called from behind the counter and waved her over.

Brandy peered at the person, then Vanessa and gave her an apologetic smile. "I'm sorry, I really need to go see what's wrong. Can we maybe continue this—"

Vanessa dismissed her. "Nah, it's okay... go! Go get to work. I'd hate for you to get fired."

Brandy's laughter lit up her face. "I'll kick his ass if he tries," she said before whispering, "One of my brothers owns it." She sent Vanessa a conspiratorial wink and rushed behind the counter.

She watched them work quickly to shorten the line that had formed. Brandy was kind, and her employees clearly respected her. Vanessa checked the time and realized she needed to get to her own shop. On Saturdays she opened before lunch and remained open until well past dinner. Her customers came from all kinds of backgrounds, and she did what she could to cater to their shopping needs.

An hour before closing, Vanessa stretched her neck from side to side and sighed. It had been a rather busy day, and while she was happy for the sales, she was beat. Leaning against the counter, she cast her eyes on her scribble. She had made notes of the items she needed to create in the coming day, aware it would involve some late nights, when the door chimed.

"Welcome! Please let me know if I can help you find anything," she said to her notebook.

"Great! Maybe you can tell us why you won't give Carter another chance."

Vanessa's head shot up as she met the curious gaze of one woman and Serena's serious expression. "Umm... What?" she muttered, unable to grasp what was happening.

The first woman offered her hand once they reached the counter. "Hi, I'm Andrea."

"Andrea," Vanessa muttered. "Oh, Andrea! You have a birthday coming up, right?"

Andrea tipped her head and smiled. "I do—oh! Was Carter in here shopping for me? Because I'd love to not get another gift card to an electronics store. Bless him, he does not know how to shop for women." Andrea faced Serena and asked, "Did I tell you he bought me a vacuum one year? A vacuum? What the hell was that? James is lucky *he* never did that shit, or I'd have bopped him on his handsome head."

"Andrea." Serena chuckled before nodding toward Vanessa. "Remember why we came?"

Andrea huffed as she took in the store before meeting Vanessa's eyes. "Yes, I remember, but dammit, there are so many pretty things in here."

"Talk first, shop later."

Vanessa blinked her eyes rapidly after moving them back and forth between the women. "Hi, Serena, was there a problem with your order?"

"Nope," she said, popping the P for added emphasis. "I just wanted to come talk to you about Carter."

"There's nothing to say," Vanessa said as she shut the notebook.

"Mhmm."

Vanessa's brows pinched together. "How many are there of you? I mean, Brandy got me at the coffee shop, and now you two…"

Andrea laughed. "Oh, honey, we're just multiplying, especially as everyone finds their soul mates. All that's left is for Edward and Carter, and that'll make fourteen of us not including kids." Vanessa's eyes rounded before she remembered Carter mentioning being one of seven. "Don't worry though. James—he's my man—Junior, who is the oldest, and Edward, who is never around won't pop by. I can't say anything for Ethan, Serena's man, or Max. The Brodericks are a pretty tight group."

"Enough."

Something strange came over Vanessa at Serena's single word, so she remained quiet after filing away the information Andrea had spewed.

"Look, we all know there is a connection between Carter and you—"

"No, you don't."

Serena glared, erasing any trace of the sweet woman who had put in a large order. "Your body doesn't light up at just his name? It didn't feel like you'd taken a nine-volt battery to your tongue at merely his touch? Your heart isn't threatening to shrivel up at just the thought of never seeing him again as we speak?"

Vanessa opened and shut her mouth a few times. She cleared her throat, and at the feel of her hands trembling, she slammed them on her hips. "Just because you came in here and made a *very* large order, doesn't give you the right to get in my business."

"*Oh,* I really like her," Andrea whispered from the corner of her mouth.

Serena placed two fingers to her temple and shut her eyes. "Help me, goddess, because I can't with these two."

Goddess?

"Look, Vanessa, I really like you, and I adore Carter. He's a really good man. It would be rather tragic if you didn't give him another shot."

She narrowed her eyes. "Did he send you here?"

Serena threw her hands up with frustration. "No, he did not. I did, however, see how *miserable* he's been since your first date exploded in your faces."

"He's miserable?" Vanessa asked before she could stop herself. Her heart did a little pitter-patter at the thought that he was as upset as she was.

Andrea scoffed. "I've known this family for a very long time. I've never seen him like this, honey. I don't know you—well, at all—and I have to admit, you two share the same dog-got-run-over-by-a-truck expression."

"But he lied to me. I can't be with someone who would lie..."

Serena reached across and held one of Vanessa's hands in hers. "Sometimes we lie to protect the people we love."

"Whoa... We just met. I'm not sure why we're bringing up the L word." She stammered, her stomach rolling with butterflies. A little voice in her head chuckled and told her meeting Carter had been love at first sight. Vanessa shook her head vehemently. "Uh-uh, no. Lies are lies. Cheating assholes lie. Criminals lie... not people who love you—er... people you claim are in love."

Serena and Andrea laughed. "Oh, people fib to their loved ones all the time to protect them," Serena stated.

"Are you kidding me? If I admitted to James the tile he laid was a smidge off, he'd rip it all up, and we'd waste money and time on a job. Nope, my ass is fibbing until I'm blue in the face."

"And when Ethan brings me a tea as a gift because he thought I'd like it and it tastes like I licked the dirt in the garden? Yeah, I'm going to lie through my teeth, so I don't break his heart and make it so he won't be thoughtful ever again."

Andrea took hold of Vanessa's free hand and gave her a soft smile. "You see, honey. There are some lies that are necessary."

Vanessa deflated. "He made me feel like I'd lost my mind."

They nodded in understanding. "It's going to happen a lot..."

She looked at them in horror.

Serena shrugged. "If it's any consolation, we make men lose their minds too."

"And for the record, only Brandy knows we're here. Carter hasn't said much," Andrea told her and squeezed her hand before releasing it. "Now, I've got some shopping to do before you close up for the night."

Serena shook her head and chuckled but held on to Vanessa's hand. "Please give him—this thing between you two—another chance. I promise you won't regret it. The Broderick men may not always be playing with a full deck, but their love is fierce."

chapter 12

The last thing Carter wanted to do was host this week's family dinner. He just wanted another night alone with a glass of whiskey and whatever action flick he landed on. He loved the crazy bunch, but slapping on a smile and a jovial mood would not work. His family would see right through the charade.

He grabbed his phone, called their favorite Italian pizza joint, and ordered five pizzas, two salads, and two pasta dishes. There was a good chance even that wasn't enough food, but he hoped it would cause the night to end early.

His week had dragged. He'd spent it analyzing and debating his date with Vanessa—what he could have done differently and what he wished he could change.

How could he feel this strongly for her without even barely knowing her?

Magic.

He groaned at the word. Magic had transformed his life since the moment he realized he was different. This thing with Vanessa was easily the first time he'd felt the urge to give it all away.

After their family learned of the secrets his parents had kept, they had been told explicitly of the dangers of humans learning. Debbie, Junior's wife, was human and had zero magic in her, but she also knew how important it was not to blabber about questionable things. Andrea, on the other hand, could also see spirits like his brother, albeit not as frequently or strongly. They could only guess the magic in her blood was diluted and minimal.

He worried about Vanessa. Who had she confided in about the things she had seen? Was there any magic in her bloodline?

His doorbell rang, drawing him from his line of thought. Carter pushed to his feet and took the time to mentally prepare for his family's loving and overbearing ways as he moved toward the door.

"Wow! You really do look like shit," Junior blurted, his face contorting with concern before he leaned forward. They pounded each other on the back. "What's wrong?"

Thankfully, Debbie pushed forward. "Ignore him. Hi, honey."

He wrapped her in a tight embrace and sucked in a calming breath filled with the scent he associated solely with Debbie. "Hi."

Releasing her, he was disappointed to see no one else had arrived. He was not in the mood to have Junior's razor-sharp attention on him. "I put in an order of pizza just a little bit ago," he said as he pushed the door closed.

"Wait up!" Brandy called, and when he pulled open the door, he saw her hauling Gia in her car seat.

"Here, gimme the princess," he said, taking the carrier from Brandy, who sighed with relief.

Rising to her tiptoes, Brandy pressed a kiss to his cheek and patted the other. "Hi, Car. I remember looking like that," she muttered before slipping past him into the house.

He opted to ignore her comment. "Where's Ryan?"

"He's getting the Pack 'n Play out of the trunk," she called over her shoulder.

Carter set the carrier down and kneeled before his niece. "Hi, baby girl! I've missed you," he said as he unbuckled her. "You won't bring up what a mess I am." He brought her to his chest and pressed his lips to the downy hair on her head.

"I think my ovaries just exploded."

Carter rose to his full height and turned. Andrea stared at him with hearts in her eyes, unlike James, who looked on with horror.

"Careful, Andrea," Carter said. "I think he might vomit."

She smacked James in the stomach. "Oh, stop it! You'll be a great dad, and you know it."

By the look on his brother's face, he did not believe her words.

"Look who we found," Ethan called, and the world quit spinning.

Carter froze in place, squeezing Gia to his chest as Ethan, Serena, and Vanessa walked in with Ryan hot on their tail. Afraid he would say the wrong thing again, Carter stared. A thousand different sentences, some intelligent and others not, flew through his mind.

Something in his chest shifted, and a joy like no other filled him at merely her presence. Gia gave a little cry, which caused him to break eye contact with Vanessa.

"Yo, how about you don't squish my baby?" Ryan called as he set the Pack 'n Play down. He hurried over and scooped the baby from Carter's arms, which left him with nothing to do with his hands.

"Why don't you try saying hi?" Serena whispered before kissing his cheek.

He nodded but still no words left his mouth.

"Edward said he needed to work late, but he promised he'd be at the next dinner," Brandy said.

"Where's Max, Claudia, and Katia?" Debbie asked.

"Running late. They were meeting with Peter about—you know," Ryan said.

The cryptic words caused Carter to narrow his eyes on his family before returning to Vanessa's confused, deer-in-headlight stare.

"I'm sorry, I thought you knew... I can leave," she said, hurt and embarrassment coating her words.

He shook his head. "No... No, don't leave. I'm just surprised is all. No one told me you were coming over, especially not after..."

Serena returned to his side and placed a hand on his arm. "I asked her to come—"

"But I thought—"

Serena shook her head and offered him a soft smile. "It's clear she's yours. I asked her to give you a second chance. Don't fuck it up."

"But y'all stressed the importance of... you know..." Could he possibly have Vanessa and let her in on the real world around them?

"What are you guys talking about?" Vanessa asked as she crossed her arms under her breasts, pushing them higher. The simple action caused his dick to stir.

"Why don't we wait for everyone else to show and then we can have a nice long chat?" Serena asked, her tone unyielding. "Introduce her to everyone."

As a high priestess, Serena demanded respect and for her commands to be followed. As his future sister-in-law, she was kind and playful. In that moment, she was their high priestess.

He nodded and offered his hand to Vanessa, needing to touch her in some form or another. When she accepted his hand, he sucked in a shuddering breath, excited to take a step in the right direction.

Her skin was a little pale, and her eyes a bit dilated. If she felt anything he did, he could blame it all on nerves. He lowered his mouth to her ear and whispered, "They're all really nice, I promise."

After introductions, he grabbed her a glass of wine, hoping to ease the turmoil within her. She raised the glass to her lips as his front door opened once again. Peering past her, he spotted Max's beaming face as he carried Katia in one arm and held Claudia's hand in the other.

"Please tell me the food is ready, because I'm about to eat this little one," Max announced before playfully nipping Katia.

Vanessa turned at the sound of Katia's giggles and squeals of delight. "Who's that?"

"Max, his fiancée, Claudia, and her daughter, Katia. Come on, I'm sure you'll like them," he said as he pressed a hand to her lower back and guided her toward them.

His family did not disappoint with their kind and welcoming nature, but he still wished he understood why Vanessa was there. Refusing to be an ass and leaving her to go find out, he stuck by her side as Katia entertained them with a story.

"Be right back," he whispered to Vanessa when the doorbell rang throughout the house. He pulled open the door and was met with a mouthwatering scent, then paid the delivery guy. As he shut the door again, he was juggling the pizzas in one hand and the bags of food in the other.

"Here, let me help you!" Vanessa told him as she hurried to his side and freed his hand of bags.

Everyone worked together and dished themselves food on the paper plates he'd retrieved from the pantry. For a moment, he regretted not ordering more but was pleased to see it was just what they needed. Little groups split off to eat and chat, leaving him leaning against the counter with Vanessa at his side.

"I'm sorry," she muttered. "I thought you knew I was coming over."

Carter swallowed his bite of food and shook his head. "Don't be. I'm really excited you're here. I wish it were just us and not all five million of my family members."

Vanessa giggled, and the sound soothed his soul. "There really are a lot of you."

He nodded and grinned as he took them all in. "They're pretty great when they're not sticking their noses in your business. Although... I'm kind of glad they did, or else you wouldn't be here now."

Vanessa gave him a teasing check of her hips before leaning her head against his arm. The simple action was sweet and comfortable. It left him wishing for more easy moments. He knew his family had a dual purpose to her invitation, but he would enjoy his time before they laid their cards out.

chapter 13

"All right, everyone," Serena called as she faced them all.

"What's going on?" Vanessa whispered to Carter, but he only shook his head and watched the beautiful redhead.

"I think it's pretty clear Carter found his match," Serena stated, and Vanessa stiffened. "We also know some conversations and observations are best kept private."

A knot formed in her belly, and heat filled her cheeks at the words. Had he told the entire family she was a lunatic? They had seemed so nice, but in that moment, she questioned if it all had been an elaborate hoax at her expense.

Carter set his plate aside and wrapped an arm around her shoulders, drawing her against his warm body. She wanted to melt into his touch, but she remained as stiff as a rod.

"Vanessa, you've made it pretty clear lies are unacceptable," Serena stated. "But some lies aren't meant to hurt others, but rather protect."

The family nodded in agreement but kept their eyes on Serena. "Ignoring this is our weekly family dinner, we're all here because it's been pretty evident that without you, Carter isn't himself."

"We barely know each other," Vanessa whispered without peering up at him.

"I'd also say you aren't the same without him," Serena said softly. "Look, you were right. He lied. His lie hurt you both, but you need to understand he skirted the truth to keep you safe."

Her words blended with the memories of the argument they'd had, and she could not seem to take a breath as she waited to hear what else Serena would say. Excitement and nerves tumbled around in her stomach.

"For some unknown reason to us, you've noticed and borne witness to events others are blind to. You aren't crazy, but I think in a moment you'll question everything you've ever known. Before the truth can be revealed, I must know the truth behind your heart. Will you two please join us up here?"

One of his brothers stood and joined Serena—Ethan, Vanessa thought was his name. The hair at the nape of her neck stood on end as the family faced him and Serena.

Carter took her hand, interlacing their fingers, and tugged her along. In a matter of seconds, they stood before Serena. "You're safe, I promise," Carter whispered near her ear, his breath sending a shiver down her neck.

Ethan offered them each a hand, and she stared down at it. Her attention moved from his palm to his face before landing on Carter's kind smile. She did not have the slightest idea what was happening or why she was overcome with the feeling she could trust Carter wholeheartedly.

Maybe she really had lost her mind, and seeing weird things in town was the least of her worries.

"I promise, family or not, if I did anything to hurt you, Carter would probably kill me for it," Ethan said, his face set with no humor evident.

Vanessa sucked in a breath before relenting and placing her free hand on his. Ethan gave them a small nod and held on tightly. No one spoke. The air around them stilled as her heart hammered away against her sternum.

When Ethan opened his eyes to take them in, she gasped and took a step back. His pupils were gone, his eyes glowing white.

Carter squeezed her hand. "Shh…. It's okay."

"Ah… I see you've found her, child."

Vanessa's eyes wanted to pop out of their sockets. Ethan's mouth moved, but the voice was not his. Rather, it sounds like a woman, an older woman.

"Be still, child. No one here will hurt you," he/she said with Ethan's creepy eyes directed at her. "You feel the soul mate bond to Carter. Trust in him. All that you have seen is true, but you've put yourself in grave danger by speaking of it."

Ethan's head turned to face the room, scanning the family as he said, "He's coming…"

"Well, ain't that some shit," Brandy muttered with a shake of her head.

Ethan released her hand, and when she met his eyes, they were normal once more. "It seems your curious nature has put you in jeopardy."

"What the hell does that mean?" Carter blurted, tugging her into his arms.

Ethan scrubbed his face. "Before letting me return, she showed me Vanessa has drawn some attention to herself."

"Fuck," Carter growled.

She pushed away from him, unable to think in his arms, and did a circle in the room. "What the hell was that?" she asked, pointing at Ethan. "And what the hell is going on?"

Someone tapped her on the shoulder, and she spun on her heels, swaying a little as she lost her balance. "You're going to want some of this, and I suggest you sit down," Andrea said, offering her a full glass of red wine.

She looked at Carter, and he gave her a nod. "Andrea's right. Come on, let's sit down."

"The short, short version…" Serena stated. "Everything you saw or have seen is not part of your imagination. You are most definitely not crazy, and neither are we. If I had to guess, somewhere in your family line, there was a witch, maybe two since most humans are oblivious to the world we live in."

Her lips parted before she smacked them together a few times. "Excuse me, did you say witch?" She raised the wine to her lips and gulped. Somehow, she had entered the twilight zone, and while she was there with the sexy-as-sin Dr. Tingles, she worried about Georgia and her family missing her.

Serena sighed with annoyance. "You know, for someone who's seen weird shit, you really are unbelieving. Brandy? Can I get some help to speed this along?"

Brandy chuckled as she passed the baby to her husband. "Vanessa, we were all in your shoes about a year ago. No, wait… Everyone in here but Ryan, Serena, and Claudia were in your shoes. I was the first, and let me tell you, it was some crazy, fucked-up shit. Falling into Wonderland kind of shit. Before I scare you…"

"Great," Vanessa muttered and took another sip, letting the wine warm her insides.

"Carter, she's not going to believe anything if you let her keep drinking," Serena stated.

Vanessa twisted, protecting the wine from his grubby fingers. "My wine!"

He chuckled and raised his hands in defense. "Brandy?"

One second Vanessa was holding the wine glass, but the next her fingers were pressed against her chest. "What the?" She turned and her brows pinched as Brandy swirled the delicious red liquid in the glass before smelling it.

"Mmm... What kind is this?" she asked Carter. "Never mind." In Brandy's free hand, the bottle and an empty glass appeared.

"Where did that—"

"Magic," Brandy said as she poured herself a glass and sipped. "Mmm... tasty!"

"Brandy," Junior warned from the side, his arms crossed over his chest and a smirk playing at his lips.

Brandy sighed and set everything down on the side table. "We're all witches. We each have different powers, and we all have soul mates. Serena is the high priestess of the local coven. Out of everyone here, I have the most powers," she said, and a ball of fire formed in her hand.

Katia clapped excitedly from Max's lap, and her mother hushed her.

The flame became a frozen ball of ice before it disappeared, and a gust of wind blew Vanessa's hair away from her face. "I can call forth all the elements and use them. Let's say mums that are dead? I can bring them back to life."

Vanessa's eyes rounded. "You? You're the one who did that?"

Brandy nodded. "I did, back when I was first learning about everything and Peter and Ryan were pretty much holding me hostage so this asshole of a demon wouldn't get me. I was out for a walk, and the flowers drew my attention. It was the first time I'd ever made something regain life."

There were so many things Vanessa wanted to address from Brandy's statement. "You can bring things back from the dead?" she blurted.

Brandy chuckled. "No one can do that."

"We don't touch that kind of magic," Serena stated firmly.

"I'd come back from the store with plants to replace the mums and thought I was hallucinating," she muttered.

Brandy's face fell. "I'm so sorry, Vanessa. I didn't know at the time how my magic could affect others."

"The red eyes you saw were most likely a tubar. Tubars are lower-level demons and more of a nuisance, but they can be very dangerous," Ryan said as he rubbed his daughter's cheek absentmindedly. "It's actually how Brandy and I officially met. One was after her, but she didn't know how to protect herself."

"What about the glowing yellow eyes?" Vanessa asked and a silent moment passed among the group. "What?"

"Not all supernatural beings are bad, as not all are good," Claudia stated. "Glowing yellow eyes are a trait of werewolves…"

"Werewolves?" Vanessa asked carefully.

"There are two types. Both typically keep to themselves, but the ones to worry about are not a part of a pack," Claudia stated before her eyes flashed a golden hue in Vanessa's direction.

Vanessa gasped, and Max pulled Claudia into him.

"We know plenty of werewolves who are as much a part of this family as the seven of us are, thanks to our blood relation," Brandy declared, and Vanessa understood the underlining warning.

"Okay, some good, some bad, others both good and family?" Vanessa offered Claudia a cautious smile.

"As you can imagine, talking about any of this in public would make you look crazy, but worse, it will put a target on your back," Serena stated. "*This* is why I wanted to have the ancestor who took over Ethan's form to verify you and Carter were indeed mates. Unfortunately, she also confirmed the worst-case scenario—"

"I have a target on my back."

Serena gave her a grim smile. "The road ahead of you and Carter will be long and bumpy. I can promise we'll do everything we can to figure out whose attention you've grabbed and eliminate the threat."

"I have a question," she said, and Serena nodded for her to continue. "What about the people I saw disappear?"

Serena shrugged. "They were probably witches. There's a spell that can hide us from view."

Vanessa nodded. "Do I have powers?" she asked and chewed on her lower lip.

"We can't say for sure, but I don't think you hold any. I do think if we followed your lineage, we'd find one or two witches."

chapter 14

Carter placed the lid onto the empty garbage can and watched Vanessa as she wiped down his island. "You're taking all of this better than I expected."

She chuckled and cast him a side glance. "My brain wants to explode with all the information."

He took the cloth from her hands and rinsed it before washing his hands. "Thanks for your help."

"Of course," she said, leaning against the counter.

Carter dried his hands and tossed the towel aside. In a few steps, he stood before her, caging her in as he placed his hands on the counter. "I really didn't mean to upset you by lying."

She shook her head. "I get this lie… I never even imagined any of this, and honestly, I'm still having a hard time processing it."

He nodded. "Sleep on it, and ask me whatever you want after."

Her gaze lowered to his mouth, and the constant hum he felt in her presence intensified. They had not discussed a second date or the announcement they were soul mates, but he could not go another minute without kissing her.

"I'm going to kiss you," he whispered as he lowered his head to hers.

Her breath fanned his lips. "Okay..."

Carter stilled as he captured her mouth. Her lips were soft and pliant under his. The faint taste of the pinot noir she'd drank earlier lingered on their soft curves. Vanessa's hands moved to his hips, and her silky tongue darted along his lower lip.

Unable to ignore the need demanding to be filled, he lost all control. His mouth crushed hers, and their tongues swept every available corner. Vanessa's nails dug into his sides as he shoved a hand into her hair, tipping her head for better access as his other one pressed against the thrumming at her neck.

The woman drove him mad. He never wanted another like he did Vanessa. Her body, mind, and soul called to him without knowing all of her. He had witnessed his siblings fall one by one, and he hadn't understood their short courting, but as his body raged against him, he finally grasped the overwhelming need they must have felt.

Carter could now better understand his primal instinct to mark Vanessa as his, but the way his brain and heart screamed *mine* without knowing the woman inside and out was ridiculous.

Pleasure and pain radiated as his dick pressed against his zipper. He pulled her closer to him. Her softness pressing against his hard lines was not enough. He wanted all of her. Her little moans drove him on, making him want to hear her cry out in ecstasy.

His name on her lips...

Carter bent and grabbed her from the backs of her thighs and set her on the counter. Her center pressed against him, and her legs wrapped around him as he pulled them flush. Pausing for a breath, he noted she was as lost in the desire suffocating them as he was.

Vanessa's hands slid up his chest and around his neck. Her fingers dove into his hair and tugged on the strands. He had never been into rough sex, but in that moment, he knew that if things continued, he would fuck her senseless.

Releasing her lips, he kissed across her face and down her neck. Carter sucked in deep breaths through his nose, hoping he could control the raw, animalistic need driving him. He had never been reckless or hurt a woman in his life, and he did not plan to start now.

"Carter," Vanessa whimpered as she ground against him.

He hissed at the electricity running along his body. Squeezing his eyes tight, he sucked on a little dip at her collar bone as he realized what he needed to do.

Tonight would be all about her.

He tugged her shirt off and made quick work of freeing her from her bottoms before setting her back on the counter.

"Oh!" she squealed. "Cold!"

He chuckled and ran his hands up her thighs. "Not for much longer," he said, his voice rough.

Carter teased her, enjoying the way her gaze darkened and her head lolled. His fingers worked her as he peppered her exposed neck with kisses.

She tasted like honey and home.

Vanessa now knew their family's truth. She did not call them crazy or run away screaming. He had not lost her, and he would do everything in his power to honor his mate.

As he spread her legs apart, his mouth watered at the sight of her swollen sex. He took his time, licking and kissing the flesh. Her fingers dug into his scalp until he flicked her clit.

"Yes! More, please give me more." She panted and leaned back on her free hand.

Carter grinned at the sight before him. Vanessa was beautiful, and he was eager to get to know more of her, inside and out.

A surge of power consumed him as his magic swirled. He kissed, licked, nipped, and fucked her with his mouth and fingers. His dick ached as it pulsed, rubbing against the fabric of his pants, wishing it was filling her and not his fingers.

Vanessa tensed, and her cry of ecstasy bounced around them. At the sound of her release, he moaned against her but did not stop, drawing every drop of pleasure he could from her body. A guttural moan vibrated through her when her limbs began to twitch.

He licked his fingers clean of her sweetness and noted the wetness inside his pants. He had not come without touching himself since he'd started puberty. Something about Vanessa made him shoot a load like it was the first time he had seen a woman's pussy.

Her eyes met his before she dropped back on the counter. "Stop looking so smug," she muttered.

Carter chuckled and pressed a kiss to her bare mound. "Can't help it. I mean, are you complaining?" he asked, one brow raised toward his hairline as he adjusted himself.

Vanessa scoffed. "Maybe I've had better."

He captured her still-swollen clit between his teeth and tugged as his tongue flicked fervently. Her body arched, and she gasped with pleasure. "You're right," he said after releasing the nub. "I'm not very good at this. I won't ever do it ag—"

"No!" Vanessa cried, her eyes wide with horror.

At the risk of being kicked in the balls, he released a lighthearted laugh, one he had not felt in a long time. Carter flicked her clit with his finger again and loved the sound she made deep in her throat. It only led his thoughts to stray to her taking him into her pretty mouth. His dick twitched, liking the path his mind had taken.

Vanessa raised her head before lowering it. "Damn, I think you broke me. I'll return the favor as soon as I'm not a limp noodle."

Carter told his body to settle at her words. "Come here, sweetheart." He helped her up and back into her clothes before scooping her into his arms. Vanessa curled into him as she wrapped her arms around his neck.

It was the most natural feeling to hold her close. He wanted to keep her there and never let go. She was his and his alone.

After years of avoiding commitment with all the wrong women, he was prepared to make things permanent with Vanessa after only hours of being in her presence. There was so much they needed to learn about each other, and that alone spoke of his mental state where she was concerned.

"What's the matter?" she whispered, her hot breath seeping through his shirt.

He lowered onto the couch and settled her on his lap. "What makes you think something's wrong?"

"You just tensed."

He chuckled. "Just thinking…"

Her head tipped back so she could look at him. "About what?"

He sighed. "Don't you think it's crazy?"

"There're lot of crazy things in this world. You're going to have to be a little more specific."

Needing the connection, he kissed her forehead. "True. I meant this pull between us. We barely know each other, and I can't seem to let you go."

Vanessa nodded against his chest. "I know what you mean. Is this how it's supposed to feel?"

"What?"

"Being soul mates or whatever?"

He squeezed her to him before shrugging. "I have no idea. Maybe?"

A moment of comfortable silence passed, and he wondered if she had fallen asleep until she murmured, "Your sister's pretty badass."

He grinned. "That she is. Brandy's definitely the strongest one of the seven of us, but I guess that's our family line. The women were all badasses. At least, that's what we've gathered."

"Everyone seems really nice," she murmured.

"Except when they're pains in the asses, getting in your business," he said, thinking of Ethan.

She chuckled. "That's Georgia."

The sound vibrated against him, and he grinned. His chest ballooned at the noise, a calm filling him.

"She's always all up in my business when she's around... but I can't imagine her any other way."

Georgia had obviously never told Vanessa the truth about her family. He was surprised, considering the length of their friendship. Carter supposed it had more to do with keeping Vanessa safe than trusting her with a secret of that magnitude.

Carter cleared his throat. "You know you can't talk to Georgia about anything you learned tonight… right?"

chapter 15

Vanessa stiffened in his arms. "Georgia would never tell anyone," she said, pushing away from him. She crossed her arms under her breasts, her sight going red at his words.

Carter scooted to the edge of the couch and placed his elbows to his knees. "I never said she'd say anything, but it doesn't matter, Vanessa. You *can't* tell her anything."

She tossed her arms in the air and spun on her heels. "You don't know her, Carter! I tell her everything and she'll take it all to her grave!"

His head dropped, chin pressing to his chest. "You still can't tell her…"

"Why the hell not? Give me one good reason!" she snapped. A part of her knew she was being unreasonable, but she did not appreciate being told what she could and could not say, especially to Georgia.

Carter's hands moved roughly through his hair, his strands sticking up with the action. She wondered what he looked like after a night of screwing. Vanessa shook her head, forcing the thought out of her mind. Sex was the least of her concerns.

The little voice in her head countered. *If he can make you forget your name with only his tongue and fingers, are you really going to take sex off the table?*

"My family invited you here tonight because of who you are to me. They decided to tell you the truth to protect you. We are trying to keep you safe, and if you tell Georgia—or anyone else for that matter—it will put *my family*... all the people I love, in danger!"

He pushed to his feet and walked away from her. His shoulders were rigid and rose with each heavy breath he took. Her instinct was to comfort him, but she could not allow it to happen.

Carter groaned and faced her. "I'm sorry, Vanessa, but it's not your secret to tell."

She was completely torn and confused. On one hand, she understood where he was coming from, but on the other, she hated being told what she could or could not say or do. It was not in her nature to bow down to anyone, let alone a man. It was why she had been single for a long stretch of time.

Walking around the couch, she felt his eyes on her.

"What are you doing?" he whispered as she dug inside her purse.

Once she found her phone, she unlocked it and pulled open the Uber app. "I'm calling for a ride," she muttered and sighed once the area around her showed no signs of a possible ride.

"Please don't go," he said, standing closer this time.

She shook her head. "I can't. I need some space..."

Vanessa: Can you pick me up?

She hit send and waited while the three little dots danced a few moments later.

Georgia: I thought you went to Carter's?

Vanessa: I did.

Before she could tap out another message, Carter placed his large hand over the screen. "I'll drive you home," he said and handed her her purse. When she raised her gaze to his, a piece of her heart twisted. He looked hurt and confused, and she wanted to fix it as much as she wanted to shake him like a ragdoll until he agreed Georgia could also know his secret.

Georgia: Wish I could, babe, but I'm not in town. I can call someone else if you'd like. What the hell happened?

Her shoulders slumped, and she nodded silently. Carter's hand on her lower back seared her through her clothes. It felt right, but she was so annoyed with the man, she wanted to rip it off and feed it to him.

Where he was concerned, her emotions flashed hot and cold. A small part of her knew she was overreacting, but the other part feared that if she backed down, it would set the stage for their relationship.

"I live in the Mandolin Apartments on Acadia and Rawly," she told him after he slid behind the wheel.

Rock music played quietly as Vanessa watched the trees pass by through the window. She breathed in the scents of leather and man. The heated seat warmed her, lulling her to sleep after her two orgasms and the adrenaline within her had plummeted.

She never argued or fought. Carter brought out a side of her she had not known she possessed. She could feel him watching her and her traitorous body came to life. With merely a glance, he warmed her like a clear summer day.

It was absurd how much she wanted this man in her life. He played her body like he'd known it all his life. Her orgasms had been one of a kind, rocking her unlike any other.

"I'm sorry, sweetheart." His soft words filled the car, even over the music. "My intention was never to insult you or Georgia, but you need to understand that simply knowing what you now know puts you in harm's way."

"Then why did you guys bother telling me?" she snapped.

He sighed. "In your case? Not knowing was far more dangerous. As it is, we now know you've attracted someone's attention…"

Her brows pinched as she was reminded what Ethan—no, the woman who had taken over Ethan—had said. *"He's coming... Together you stand; apart you'll fall."*

"How accurate has Ethan or that... woman been? I mean, how do you really know I'm in danger?"

Carter ran a hand down his face and sighed. "Ethan's pretty good with his powers. The woman is an ancestor who takes over him. As I drive you home, everything in me is screaming to bring you back to my place. I don't like this at all, sweetheart. Something isn't right, but I also have a feeling if I don't drive you home, it'll drive a huge wedge between us."

She bit her lip and stared through the windshield. Vanessa would not admit that every mile closer to her apartment felt wrong. Acknowledging it to herself was bad enough. She was tired of feeling like a crazy person.

His phone chimed with a text, and the screen lit the inside cabin. He pressed the screen on his entertainment center and a robotic voice filled the car. "You have a text from—" Carter sighed while his car slowly read the digits of the unknown number, and Vanessa stiffened at his side.

"Who sent that?" she asked.

Carter looked from the road to her to the phone before returning his gaze to the road. He scoffed. "No idea."

She pressed her lips together firmly and crossed her arms. They were sucking at being supposed soul mates. Their communication was shit, and secrets still loomed over them like angry clouds threatening to soak them.

He turned into the complex and she guided him to her building, where he found an open spot and parked.

"Thanks for bringing me home," she said and pulled the handle. The door was still locked, so she slid her free hand along the door panel in search of the lock. "Want to give me a hand?"

"Vanessa?"

She paused at the sound of her name rolling off his tongue. His tone was hesitant and cautious, drawing her attention more than an angry one ever could.

"I don't feel right leaving you here. Wait," he said, raising a hand when her lips parted to argue with him. "I have a spare bedroom, and you're welcome to use it if you want to get some of your things, at least until we can figure out whose radar you landed on."

His concern was evident. He seemed to have aged ten years since their date. She shook her head. "I appreciate your concern, but I'll be fine."

Carter's lips formed a straight line, telling her without words he did not agree. With his eyes still on hers, he unlocked the door. She broke the connection, a tiny shard twisting in her heart as she turned her back on a man she already cared deeply for.

With a shake of her head, she sent the thought away and exited the car. He met her at the back, his hands shoved in his pockets, shoulders bunched with tension, and the muscles in his jaw twitching.

"You don't need to—"

Carter glared at her. "Let's get you inside."

Side by side, they walked in silence to her second-floor apartment. "Well, thank you for…" She considered saying "everything," and "nothing," and a slew of other things but left the sentence hanging.

"I want to check inside before I leave," he stated, and something told her to not fight him on it.

She offered him a small nod and unlocked the door. Vanessa turned the doorknob and flipped on the light. Her apartment was the same as it had been hours ago, yet so much in her life had changed.

"Who lives there?" Carter asked, his gaze trained on Tyler's door.

"Tyler. The guy I brought in with the dog bite."

Carter gave a short nod and followed her in as she thought of what to say in light of everything she'd learned. "That *was* a dog bite, right?"

He studied her modest apartment. "No, and if you hadn't brought him in when you did, he'd be dead," he said matter-of-factly.

Her gaze widened with surprise before narrowing. Carter's hands were in the air, and symbols and words were forming around her windows. She rubbed her eyes and watched him repeat the same actions at each window before stopping at her door.

She should ask what he was doing, or hell, he should have asked her first, but she could not form the words. Magic was real… She could not believe it. She had witnessed some phenomenal things at his house with his sister showcasing her power, but somehow what Carter was doing felt different. Maybe it had more to do with *Carter* than anything else.

"The wards should help keep you safe inside the apartment until we can figure out who the threat is," he said.

"Wards? That's what—" She raised her hand up and down in the direction of where she had seen the images before they disappeared. "What that was?"

He nodded. "If you need anything, don't hesitate to ask." Neither spoke as Carter studied her for a moment. "Vanessa, I know all of this is crazy and new to you, but if you get anything out of it, know this. You're my soul mate. I know you feel it too. There isn't anything I wouldn't do for you."

All the air seeped out of her lungs at his words. She nodded her understanding and watched him open the door.

"Lock this behind me," he demanded and then he was gone.

chapter 16

Carter waited by the door until he heard the deadbolt slide into place. He hated leaving her. It felt unnatural and wrong. He stepped toward the stairs but paused at the top and looked at Tyler's door. He had not sensed the man's magic when he treated him, but facing the door, Carter noted magic in the air.

He did not know if having Tyler, a fellow witch, as his mate's neighbor was good or bad. Without knowing the man, Carter could not put Vanessa's life in Tyler's hands. As it was, Carter did not want to leave her in anyone's care.

He slid his phone out of his back pocket and called the unknown number that had threatened him by text. Carter jogged down the flight of stairs and spoke when the call was answered. "Georgia?"

"What the fuck did you do now?" she snapped.

He shook his head. "I told her she couldn't tell you my secret, and now my mate's pissed off with me."

"Huh?" she asked. The sound of papers shuffling filtered through the line.

"Hold on," he said and slid into his car. "My family and I told her everything."

She gasped. "Everything?"

He rolled his eyes. "She doesn't know about *you*. She did, however, want to tell you about me. Now that she knows, I suspect you're going to have to walk through fire after keeping this from her all along if she does find out about you."

"Fuck!" she snapped, and something in the background crashed.

He scrubbed his face with a hand. "Look, we have bigger problems where she's concerned."

"Bigger? How's that? You just told a human about our world?"

He ignored her words and smirked. "You know all about my family?"

"Yeah, for the most part."

"Do you know about Ethan's ability?"

Georgia cleared her throat. "He can see the future or some shit?"

"It's more complicated than that. Sometimes he's used as a vessel by ancestors needing to pass on a message."

"Creepy," she mumbled.

He nodded, even though she could not see it. Ethan's ability was constantly adapting, and he agreed with Georgia's sentiment. "Well, look, tonight he not only confirmed Vanessa and I are soul mates, but her curious nature has landed her on *someone's* radar."

If not for the seriousness of the situation, Carter would have laughed at the creative string of swear words Georgia tossed out. A man stepped out of a car and moved toward Vanessa's building. Carter leaned forward, hugging the steering wheel to his chest as he watched.

"Carter?" Georgia snapped, her tone letting him know she had called his name a few times.

"Hold on," he said and watched the man let himself in the apartment below Tyler's. He sucked in a breath and leaned back in his seat. "Sorry, just needed to see where someone was going."

"Wait a minute. Are you still at her apartment complex?"

"Yeah. I'm in my car watching over her."

"You realize how stalkerish that sounds, right?"

His brows pinched with frustration. "What the hell would you have me do, Georgia? Someone's after her, and she's fucking vulnerable to our world. She refused to stay at my place, and I can't let anything happen to her."

"This is why I hope I never meet my mate," she muttered.

"That's messed up, considering we both know your males can't have sex until they do."

"Not my problem."

His phone beeped, alerting him of an incoming call. "Let me call you back. Someone's calling."

He noted the caller ID and answered. "Hey, Peter."

"Yo," he said by way of greeting. "Brandy called. Seems you Brodericks can't seem to stay out of trouble. Congrats on finding your mate."

"Thanks."

"Now, how can I help? I hear someone's coming after her, but we don't know who," Peter said.

Carter gave Peter a rundown of everything, exhaustion setting in after repeating the story once more.

"So, we have a human soul mate this time, now she knows about our world, and because she opened her mouth at the wrong time, someone's got her on their radar. Fuck, y'all really need to find your mates in less dramatic ways."

"No shit…"

"What's her name?"

"Vanessa Rayne."

Peter made a noise on the other end of the line. "Rayne. Vanessa Rayne. Why does that sound familiar?"

He sighed, knowing he would be getting another earful. "Georgia?"

"Georgia?" he asked. "*Oh,* well shit. Little Vanessa Rayne is your mate? I haven't seen her since she was a teen. We warned Georgia to drop her, but she refused, promising our secret was safe. Even did an oath promise."

"Oath promise?" Carter asked.

"She literally can't tell Vanessa the truth about herself. If she breaks the promise, she'll be shunned by the pack and on her own."

Carter whistled. "That's rather harsh."

"It's pack," Peter stated firmly. "Pack law is something you'll never understand."

"Obviously," he muttered.

Peter sighed. "Things are different with Vanessa, now that we know she's your mate. Georgia still can't say anything, and I'm sure by now you've realized she'd die for Vanessa. Those two have been thick as thieves since they met. So, we don't know who the threat is or if they figured out where she lives? My guess is whoever it is, is probably a demon. They tend to get their panties all up in a bunch when a human learns about our world. I'm guessing it's because it makes it harder for them to sucker humans when they know the truth."

"All right, do you have a plan? Brandy suggested keeping Vanessa at my place, but—"

Peter's deep laughter gave Carter pause. "Brandy suggested holding Vanessa hostage? Pot meet fucking kettle. That woman…"

"Well, she never said hostage," Carter said, frowning at the thought.

"No, she didn't because that's wrong. Keeping Vanessa close—like Ryan and I did with Brandy—is the way to go. Why isn't she at your place?"

Carter recapped the events from only an hour ago. "So I set up wards in her apartment, and now I'm sitting watch."

"Smart move with the wards, but, Carter, you're not Ryan. You have a job that relies on you. You can't spend every waking moment by her without, A, freaking her out and, B, losing your job. Georgia can't be there right now either. I have her out on assignment, which means I'll either have to bring in someone to tail her or I'll have to break the news to Vanessa."

"But won't that shun Georgia?" he asked, expressing concern over the snarky werewolf best friend of his mate.

Peter chuckled. "Aw, you and Georgia becoming BFFs?"

"Shut up, you ass. I can't get on Vanessa's good side by having her best friend kicked out of her pack."

"You're a good man, Carter. Don't worry about Georgia. The oath promise only matters if Georgia says something. Once I'm done talking to Vanessa, Georgia will be free of it."

Relief filled him. Pushing Georgia away would only make him lose Vanessa, but in the short time he'd known Vanessa, he found the infuriating werewolf to be a friend. Losing Georgia would devastate both of them, and he could not do that to the women.

"Sounds good then."

"Do you work tomorrow? If so, I can get someone out there to watch her apartment for you."

He shook his head, then remembered Peter could not see it. "No, I'm off tomorrow."

"All right. If you need anything before then, just give me a call. Be safe," Peter said, and Carter gave him his good-byes before ending the call.

He called Georgia back and raised the phone to his ear.

"Please tell me she changed her mind about your place," Georgia said by way of greeting.

He chuckled. "I wish. That was Peter who called."

"Shit," she muttered.

"Short story? Tomorrow he'll go with me to Vanessa's, and we'll drop the information bomb. Not sure why you didn't bother telling me about the oath promise."

"I couldn't."

He sighed. "I understand," he said, even though he really did not. Werewolf law and procedures were something he knew little of.

"Damn it, she's going to be so pissed at me," Georgia muttered, and for the first time, he heard the devastation on her voice at the potential fallout.

"She loves you and will forgive you once everything is explained," he told her, trying to ease some of her worry.

Georgia laughed. "You have a lot to learn about our favorite human."

After agreeing, he promised to update her on the situation tomorrow. Carter ended the call and dropped it back in the cupholder. He was exhausted after the emotional rollercoaster of a day he'd had. He watched a light go out in Vanessa's apartment and peered down at his watch. It was twenty after ten. He hoped at least one of them would get a good night's rest and he knew it would not be him, not even in the luxurious soft leather seat. Reclining back, he did his best to get more comfortable.

chapter 17

Vanessa rolled to her toes and reached for the ceiling as she stretched. Dropping down on her heels, she sighed and let her head fall to one shoulder and then the next. She'd slept like crap. She grabbed her towel and headed for the bathroom, hoping the water would wake her up.

She scrubbed her body from top to bottom and rinsed the suds before shutting off the water. Feeling a fraction better, she dried and wrapped the towel around her, then pinched it under her arms.

Remembering the night before, she peeked out her blinds and spotted Carter's car. At first she was pissed to see he had not actually left when she had closed the blinds for bed. After much thought, she realized her heart warmed at the fact he'd stayed.

He said he wanted to keep her safe, and his actions proved it.

She had questioned her words and decisions until exhaustion took over. Her worries seeped into her dreams, a faceless form coming after her and Carter becoming injured in order to save her. She could still feel the agony of losing him in her dreamworld.

Padding to her kitchen in only a towel, she set her coffee pot to brew and hurried back. She dressed in record time as she scoured her brain for the right words to say. Vanessa knew she should apologize for being so bitchy, but she refused to apologize for demanding all the truth.

She refused to live with lies. Lies had the potential to destroy so much. The pull between her and Carter was real and strong. She did not want anything to come between it, including them.

Grabbing her phone, she noted Georgia never replied or called after Vanessa had sent a vague text about her fight with Carter. She frowned. It was unlike her friend to not be there when she needed her.

Instead, she closed the text window and opened one for Carter.

Vanessa: Want some coffee?

Carter: You'd be my hero.

She set the phone down and removed a second mug. With each passing second, her nerves made her crazier. She was eager to see him but afraid of what would come after everything had been said—and not said—the night prior.

Vanessa walked to the door and laid a hand on it. A strange energy pulsed around the knob, and she instinctively knew it was Carter's ward, the ward he'd put in place to protect her. Hell, he had stayed in his car all night, so why had he put the ward in place?

A knock on the other side sounded, and she yipped in surprised. Her hand flew to her chest, and she gasped for air as she tried taking a fortifying breath. She unlocked the door and pulled it open. "Hi."

His jaw was a shade darker with the overnight stubble that had grown. His eyes brightened as they took her in, one side of his mouth tipping up. Even past the exhaustion marking his face, he was gorgeous.

"Hi," he whispered.

Vanessa stepped back, and he followed her in. "I'm not sure how you take your coffee."

"Black and one scoop of sugar. May I use your restroom first?" he asked.

She showed him to the bathroom off her bedroom and returned to their mugs. Her heart beat rapidly against her sternum. A part of her felt soothed at his nearness, but the other created a mess of sugar on her countertop.

Vanessa felt him in the entry to the kitchen as she brushed the sugar into her sink. "If I'd had known you would sleep in your car all night, I would've offered the couch," she said, keeping her hands busy.

"Your apartment complex gets pretty busy after two. Did you know that?"

She turned on her heels, a mug in hand as she cocked her head to the side. Carter leaned against the frame, his arms over his chest and one ankle crossed over the other.

He looked comfortable in her space, and it sent a sizzle of electricity along her skin.

"Excuse me?" she muttered, begging her brain to stay on track.

He chuckled and pushed off the wall to accept his coffee. "Your neighbor downstairs gets a lot of visitors after two in the morning," he said and brought the coffee to his lips.

"Thank God I had my windows shut then," she muttered before sipping her latte. "Come on, we can sit on the couch."

"Do you open today?" he asked.

"You mean the shop?" she asked, fixing the pillow at her back.

"Yeah."

She nodded. "I will, but today we open around lunch."

Carter sighed and looked around her apartment. She tried to see it through his eyes. It had two side tables and an entertainment system with her TV, Blu-Ray player, sound system, and a few novels. A few mermaid figurines completed the space that she had decorated with a beachy feel.

"Are mermaids real?" she blurted.

Carter pursed his lips. "I haven't got the faintest idea. Maybe."

She pouted, wishing he knew.

He grabbed her free hand in his and squeezed. "I asked a friend over to get rid of the last of the secrets between us."

Worry pulled down his lips, and another piece of her fell for him. "Really?" she asked.

He nodded. "Sweetheart, keeping anything from you hurts. This truth will hurt you some, but I promise if you listen, you'll understand why you were kept in the dark."

She pulled her hand back and cradled the mug between her hands. "That's like a parent beating their kid and telling them it hurts them more than the kid."

Carter pushed to his feet and looked around her things. "My mom died giving birth to Brandy."

Vanessa gasped. "I'm so sorry—"

"It turns out the same thing happened to my mother and her mother's mother for a total of seven generations. Each woman died giving birth to their seventh child, a girl. That truth had been kept from us. Until Brandy's powers unbound on her twenty-first birthday, none of us knew the truth. As a young boy, I thought something was wrong with me. I even questioned if I was adopted and maybe my real parents were aliens." He turned and faced her as he chuckled. "Never in my wildest dreams would I have considered what I could do was magical."

"What can you do?" she whispered.

He looked at her door before meeting her eyes. "I heal people."

She shrugged. "All doctors do."

Carter smirked. "We do, but that I know of, they can't bring someone back from near death within moments. I told you last night, Tyler was about to die. If I had not been in the lobby saying good-bye to those ladies, he *would* be dead."

Vanessa's mouth formed an O, and he continued. "I don't work at Schwab Memorial. I used to, but now I work at Sacred Heart Hospital and Maple Valley medical group. I was only at Schwab because I was consulting on a patient with a rare pulmonary disease. I truly believe it was our fate to meet in that moment. I also thought he was your boyfriend, which is the only reason I managed to keep my mouth shut and not ask for your number right then."

Warmth crept up her neck and to her cheeks.

Carter set down his mug on a side table. "This thing between us we can't fight, and honestly I don't want to fight it now that I've found you. Secrets have no place in a relationship. I get we've only just met weeks ago, but we have a ways to go to get to know each other."

Someone knocked on the door, and he moved to it faster than she could push herself off the comfortable cushions. Carter looked out the peephole before he looked at her seriously.

"Please keep an open mind and heart. I won't lie and tell you this won't rock your world because I'm sure it will. It will piss you off most likely, but know secrets were kept for a reason," he said before pulling open her door.

Vanessa reached his side and looked from Peter to Carter before turning back to Peter. "Peter? Is Georgia okay?"

"Let him in, sweetheart," Carter stated as he tugged on her arm lightly.

"Georgia's fine, Vanessa. Hey, Carter," he said, and the men shook hands.

She looked from one to the other. "Wait... You two know each other? How do you two know each other?" she asked, her eyes narrowed on them.

Peter closed the door behind him. "Why don't we sit down?"

Carter's warm hand pressed on her lower back, and he guided her back to the couch. He sat first and helped her to his side.

Peter joined them and smiled. "I hear congratulations are in order."

Now she really felt confused. "Congratulations?"

Peter waved a hand between Carter and her. "You two? Together? An item? Fate? Soul mates? Destiny?"

She faced Carter. "*He* knows?"

Carter put an arm around her shoulders and pulled her against him. "Keep an open mind, sweetheart." He kissed her temple before telling Peter, "Why don't you get started before she vomits from nerves?"

"Hey! I don't vomit from nerves!" Vanessa replied.

Peter chuckled, drawing her attention back to the large man. He made her apartment feel so small. She barely fit on the couch with Carter to her right and Peter to her left. "All right, all right. First things first, a reminder," he said, his voice deep and radiating a power she never noticed before. "You are to repeat none of what I'm about to share with you, am I clear?"

A shiver of fear trickled down her spine. This man could break her in two, and not in the sexy kind of way she wanted Carter to. Authority and strength came off Peter in waves. He was not a man to be trifled with.

Vanessa leaned into Carter. "Yes…" She inwardly groaned at the tremble in her single word. Her stomach rolled, and she handed Carter her mug to set on the side table.

The cushions next to her shifted. "Look at me, Vanessa."

Something about his tone and words made her want to do anything but look at him. With her eyes cast down on her lap, she was thankful for Carter's presence. She had never believed a woman needed a man, but damn if it was not more comfortable with him at her side.

Sucking in a breath, she forced her spine to straighten before meeting Peter's gaze—his very-much-glowing-yellow gaze. She froze, and her lower jaw unhinged at the sight. Her mind flitted through all the information she had been given the night prior, but she failed at holding on to a single thought.

"I'm the Alumbra werewolf pack alpha, Vanessa," Peter stated before his eyes switched back to normal.

She blinked her eyes a few times before turning toward Carter. "Did I just…"

He chuckled, and she was tempted to elbow him in the gut. "Yes. His eyes glowed yellow for a few moments because he's a werewolf."

She twisted in her seat and sucked in another breath, determined to keep herself calm. "Can I see all of you?"

Peter chuckled, and Carter growled at her side as his arm dropped from her shoulder to her waist and drew her impossibly closer to him.

"Careful, we don't want Carter to get any ideas and turn me into a cat," Peter said jokingly, as if he'd told her he was going for a stroll and not his status as alpha to a werewolf pack.

Alpha. Werewolf pack.

"Wait, can you do that?" she asked, meeting Carter's serious gaze.

His face softened at the question before he looked at Peter. "I'm not sure, but I'll figure it out soon if this conversation doesn't get moving."

"You'll have to excuse him. It's hard to fight the protective streak when it comes to your mate, at least that's what I'm told. I'm sure you'll understand how he's feeling right now when the first single female gets near him."

"You don't have a mate?" she asked Peter.

A shadow crossed his face. "I don't."

Carter's grip around her waist loosened. "Why don't we talk about the elephant in the room?"

Peter nodded. "Look, pipsqueak... You're in real danger from what I hear. The worst of it is that we have no idea *who* poses this danger. The Brodericks have already let you in on their secret to protect you. As a human, you are more curious than the rest of us. It's your observant and curious nature that flagged you. There are plenty of supernatural beings who aren't keen to having humans know about them. Carter has let me know that my secret and my pack's secret needed to come out too. It wasn't his place to tell you. As part of that, there is another special person in your life who was unable to share her secret with you..." He said the last part slowly, giving her brain a moment to catch up.

Secrets. Place to tell. Special person in your life. Secrets.

Her brain processed his words in fragments before a bulb turned on in her head. The reason she even knew Peter was thanks to Georgia. *Is Georgia hiding something from me?* she wondered.

"Georgia?" she whispered, confusion coating the name.

Peter nodded and lowered to a knee before her. Even with his size, she found herself looking up. "Yes, pipsqueak. You see, long ago when you two refused to end your friendship—"

"Excuse me?" she blurted.

"Georgia was forced into taking an oath promise," he said, ignoring her. "If she broke this promise, she would be shunned from the pack and forced out."

"And what was this promise about?" she asked, shifting in her seat as her nerves wound her tighter.

Peter shrugged. "She was forbidden from ever telling you she was a werewolf."

Vanessa's face blanched, and her heart skipped a beat. The words swirled around her mixing with everything else from the last two days. "Georgia... a werewolf?"

Peter nodded but said no more. Unable to sit still, Vanessa pushed to her feet and slipped by the large man. She paced her small living room as she considered the new information bomb dropped on her lap. Carter's previous words came to mind, mixing with the revelation until she stopped in front of him.

"Georgia's a werewolf, and you knew but you didn't think to tell me?" Her words fell flat, hurt filling her.

Pain filled his eyes. "Sweetheart, it wasn't my secret to tell."

She narrowed her eyes on Peter. "And apparently it wasn't Georgia's secret to tell either," she hissed. "Does Georgia really work as a ranger, or is it some ruse for werewolf secret squirrel shit?"

Peter chuckled at her heated words. "No, she's really a ranger, but sometimes she has to go because of an order I've given."

Vanessa paused, thinking on her friend, their friendship, and their ups and downs. "Was Reni a werewolf too?" she asked of Georgia's deceased brother.

"Her whole family is full of werewolves. This is hereditary. Our bite doesn't turn anyone, but rather it kills," Peter said. "Reni was a hero who died in battle. His loss has been painful for the entire pack."

"What battle?" she asked. "Reni wasn't in the military."

"A few months back, my brother's mate was found. She escaped an awful man's grasp, but we had to go in and save other women held hostage. Reni died in the process of us trying to free those women. His death was quick, so I wasn't able to heal him," Carter stated in an even tone.

She cocked her head. "Heal him? Because you said you're a healer?"

Carter nodded and rose to his feet. He moved to her kitchen and returned with a small paring knife she used on fruit.

As he moved the blade to his forearm, Vanessa hurried to his side and pulled it back. "What the hell are you doing?"

He smiled, his face going soft and his gaze penetrating hers. "It's okay, trust me," he whispered.

Letting him go, she watched in horror as he slid the blade across the smooth skin. A thin red line formed at the shallow cut. He shifted the knife to his other hand

and laid his free hand over the wound. When she wiped the blood away, she noticed no cut remained.

"Holy shit!"

chapter 18

Anxiety filled Carter as warm water sprayed his back. He scrubbed his arms and chest, his mind on Vanessa.

The rest of their meeting with her had gone better than he could have hoped, especially after demonstrating his healing powers. After Peter left, they talked and even cuddled on the couch.

Vanessa was a strong woman, like his sister, and she did not appreciate being kept in the dark. He could not blame her either.

Carter walked her to her shop when it was time and set up wards as she prepared the store for opening. He managed to stick around for a couple hours before she kicked him out. Thankfully, Peter had sent someone to keep watch over the boutique, so Carter could go home and rest.

He tossed and turned but slept for a few hours. His time long ago in the ER had trained him for nights with little sleep. After giving up on more shuteye, he cleaned up and picked her up for dinner after the shop closed.

The woman was funny, smart, and unbelievably kind. Their dinner went smoother with no secrets between them. Not wanting to add any more attention to her, they agreed not to discuss anything magical in public.

Carter shut off the water and ran a towel over his body before grabbing his phone.

Carter: You've got eyes on her?

Peter: Man, like I told you twenty minutes ago, I put Xander on this. He's pissed about it, but he will keep her safe today. Go to work!

He set his phone on the counter and sighed. Ignoring the tightness in his stomach, he dressed for a day of patient appointments and reviewing test results. Once his outward appearance fully contradicted his mental appearance, he went to the kitchen and poured himself a to-go cup of coffee.

Carter: Please tell me we're closer to knowing who's going after Vanessa.

After slipping his phone, wallet, and keys into his pocket, he placed the strap to his bag over his shoulder and headed for the door. Thinking on his upcoming workload, he was thankful he wasn't scheduled in the ICU.

He squeezed the steering wheel in his hands, the music filling the car yet doing nothing to soothe his rough edges. Releasing a breath, he reminded himself outpatient care or not, his patients expected and deserved one hundred and ten percent of the best possible care he could provide them. His personal issues were just that, his.

Twenty minutes later, he parked in his spot and unlocked his phone.

Ethan: Working on it...

"Fucking hell," he muttered, frustration consuming him.

Carter collected his things and went inside. He knew his family and friends would do everything to keep Vanessa safe, but he hated every minute. His mate was in danger, and he could not do anything but go to work and wait.

The waiting was going to kill him. Unlike some of his siblings, he did not have the benefit of telekinesis to protect her. Carter had never been a fighter, and he regretted it then. Scuffling with his brothers would not be enough to keep a supernatural being from exacting some form of punishment on Vanessa.

"Maybe Serena can help," he mumbled.

"What?" his nurse asked, accepting the file in his hand.

Carter shook his head. "Sorry, working a problem in my head."

His day became progressively worse. He got through his patients with minimal annoyance, but by the sideways glances his staff directed at him, he must have been more of a bear than normal.

"Anyone else?" he asked.

"No."

He nodded. "Once y'all are done, close up and head home," he said and started toward his office.

"He needs to get laid," one nurse muttered softly.

"No shit. Something crawled up his ass. He's never like that," another replied as he stepped into his office.

Carter did not blame them for their comments. He would let it slide this once, but he made a mental note to both talk to them about being careless with their words around patients and to work harder at compartmentalizing his life. Sitting in his chair, he pulled up his last patient's file and then unlocked his phone.

Carter: How's your day going?

He set it down and typed out a few additional notes before saving the file. Carter looked at his schedule for the week and sighed. His poor staff had a few more crappy days ahead of them if he could not get himself sorted.

His phone vibrated loudly on the wood desk. His heart raced, and he grinned at the sight of her name.

Vanessa: Busy, thanks to more of Serena's customers coming by. Yours?

Carter: Long. Any chance you'll be up for dinner?

Vanessa: I need to work late after closing. I have some items I need to finish.

Carter: I'll bring you some food so you can focus on working. Tacos?

Vanessa: I wouldn't dare say no to tacos!

Carter: Can't wait to see you, sweetheart.

Leaning back in his chair, he sucked in a deep breath. He'd dated many women, but none of them had ever fit. Some wonderful women had come into his life and he'd had to be the asshole passing on them. One ex had even recommended him to his current hospital admin, allowing him to change hospitals and work with the best of his field in the area—an opportunity that would have taken years to sow. But now, he'd finally found the mythical woman who had slid right into his heart.

This woman did not care he was a doctor, unlike the one-night stands who wanted more so they could be a doctor's wife. She valued her business as much as he valued his. She was a woman he vowed to keep safe as long as he had breath in his lungs.

Knowing what he needed to do, he pushed to his feet after securing his computer. The office was quiet, and he made a mental note to do something kind for his staff.

The warm sun seeped into his skin as he loosened the tie around his neck. He tossed his things into the trunk, dropped his tie on top of his bag, and rolled up his sleeves, then he slid into his leather seat and pressed the car on.

Carter cranked up the music, hoping to drown his thoughts, and drove toward Sage Beginnings. The drive was easier than the one to work that morning. The extra cars in the parking lot warned him she had customers.

The bell chimed, announcing his arrival.

"Welcome to Sage Beginnings! Look around and let us know if you need any help," a woman said. He'd never seen her before, but her kind smile was welcoming and soothed some of his nerves.

He looked around for flowy auburn hair but frowned when he only found a man flipping through a book and two women discussing the stones before them.

"How can I help you?" the woman asked as he approached her.

Carter glanced around again before offering her a pathetic smile. "I'm a little bit out of my realm here, and I was actually hoping to speak with Serena."

"Oh, I'm sure I can help, unless there was a specific thing you needed from her?" she asked.

He grinned. "I'm Ethan's brother, Carter."

"Oh…*oh!* Let me go tell her—" She paused and offered someone behind him a smile. "I'll be right back."

Carter placed a hand over hers. "I don't want to take you away from your customers. If it's okay with you, I can go in the back or up to the apartment to find her."

The woman bit the corner of her lower lip as she considered her options, and Carter realized she was not sure of his identity. He removed his wallet from his back pocket and pulled out his driver's license. "See, Carter Broderick. I'm who I say I am."

"Sorry, I've just never seen you before, and well, only Max has come by."

Carter nodded as he chuckled. "Well, in case you didn't know, there are a total of seven of us."

He offered the man behind him an apologetic smile and walked to the curtain hiding the store from the back room. The room was empty, so he continued to the stairs leading up to the apartment. "Serena?" he called, hoping not to scare the high priestess.

"Carter?" she answered, confusion clear in her voice.

"Yeah!" he said, reaching the top of the stairs.

Serena kissed his cheek and smiled. "What do I owe the pleasure of two visits from my soon-to-be brother-in-law?"

He chuckled. "Well, I was hoping you could help me with something."

"Would you like some tea?" she asked, waving a hand toward the kitchen.

Carter shook his head. "No, not this time."

She nodded and waved him toward the couch. "Okay, how can I help?"

He sat next to her but near the edge of the couch. Placing his elbows on his thighs, he clasped his hands and sighed. "As you know, my mate, Vanessa, attracted some danger. As of right now, my sole power is healing. I have no way to protect her."

"You know how to set up protection wards, don't you?"

"Well, yes, but I was hoping I could do *more,*" he said, pinching his lips together.

She nodded. "I see. Well, you are a witch, so there are of course spells you can learn. I understand you haven't been given telekinesis or other powers like your other siblings?"

He shook his head. "I haven't. I honestly hadn't cared until now."

She laid a hand on his forearm. "It's okay to feel helpless, but don't worry. You've come to the right person," she said and winked.

He chuckled and offered her his thanks. Serena excused herself and slipped down the stairs. As he scooted back on the couch, his gaze landed on stones similar to the ones two women downstairs had been looking at. He reached forward and plucked one from the coffee table in front of him and turned it around in his hands.

"Black tourmaline. It's a stone used for protection as well as for grounding. You can have it if you'd like," Serena said as she placed a few items on the table next to it.

"Can I give it to Vanessa?" he asked.

"Of course. That is actually a really good idea. I'll make sure to get you a couple more from downstairs. One for her apartment, her boutique, and a small one you can keep in your pocket."

He nodded. "What's all of this?"

"You have magic in your blood but haven't been given certain powers. Sometimes using herbs and stones helps to draw out magic and aid in spell work. So, for example, Ethan can move this stone from this side of the table to the other, but you can't, right?"

"Right."

"Well, I'm going to teach you a work-around that will enable you to tap into your magic. These items will reinforce the magic so you can do it. You won't be able to do it as easily or often as those who can naturally, but then again, you Brodericks keep me on my toes regarding the norm of us witches."

He grabbed her wrist and met her eyes. "Thank you, Serena. You've been a lot of help, and my brother's really lucky to have you."

She smiled and he released her. "We're lucky to have each other."

chapter 19

Carter: I'm running later than I planned. Hope you're hungry. Bringing enough tacos for an army!

Vanessa read the text and grinned. She set the phone down to the right of her workstation and rolled her shoulders. Music played quietly from the speakers in the boutique, and the doors had been locked for nearly two hours.

Diving into her work as soon as she closed helped her not think about Carter or the million ways things had changed for her.

She grabbed the finished bracelets and carried them to their display before returning for the matching earrings. If she had known how popular the stones would be, she would have created more a long time ago.

Vanessa froze when an uneasy feeling washed over her. She turned her head slowly and found a man watching her through the glass from the sidewalk. His eyes narrowed before flashing red. She stepped back, and her gaze darted to the locked door. He gave her a sickening smile as another man sneaked up on him.

Looking at the street, she noticed it was unnaturally empty. A flash of red pulled her attention, and flames formed where the man—the thing—had stood and disappeared as fast as it began. The other man gave her a curt nod and moved into the shadows before she could nod back.

"What the hell was that?" she muttered, her heart hammering away.

A banging at the back sounded, and she yelled with surprise. She turned from the front to the back a few times before creeping upon her back door.

"Vanessa? Are you okay?"

"Vanessa? Goddamn it, let me in!"

She finally made out Carter's voice through the ringing in her ears. Her fingers fumbled as she tried to unlock the door. Swinging it open, she was relieved to see his face and tossed her arms around his neck.

His warmth pressed against her front as he guided her inside. "Shh… What happened, sweetheart? Why'd you scream?"

She put her forehead to his chest and blindly swatted his side. "You freaking scared me!"

"*I* scared you? Why? You knew I was on my way," he said, setting her back so he could close the door.

"Carter?" a deep voice called before Carter opened the door again.

Vanessa stared at the man from minutes before. He was tall, muscular, and there was a hardness about him that she could not put her finger on.

"Oh, hey, Xander!" he said, shifting a bag from one hand to the other so he could offer it. "Everything okay?"

His head made the barest movement. "Tubar, up front. I took care of it, but there are a lot more on this side of town than normal."

Tubar. She scoured her brain for what it was. Vanessa remembered hearing the name, but with everything she had learned, it was hard pinpointing it all.

"Lower level demon," Carter told her before facing Xander. "Thanks, man, I appreciate it."

"You got a dagger on you in case another shows?" Xander asked.

Carter removed a small knife from the pocket of his hoodie—a hoodie that was too warm for their current weather, paired with cargo shorts and flip flops. "Got one."

"Okay, good. You kill one before?" Xander asked.

Carter shook his head.

"Fastest kill is to pierce their heart."

Carter nodded, and she broke out into a fit of giggles. Both men turned toward her with concern evident on their faces.

"Sweetheart?"

She raised a hand before covering her mouth and laughing. "S-sorry, it's just the nonchalant way you two talk about killing someone is rather unnerving."

"It's not a someone. It's a some*thing,*" Xander stated, his tone hard.

Vanessa's laugh died on her lips. She cleared her throat and replied, "Yes, sorry."

Xander faced Carter, dismissing her and her outburst. "I'm heading out now that you're here, but Peter's sending someone else. I just don't know who."

His statement made ten different questions pop in her mind, but she bit her tongue from speaking again, at least not while the crabby man was around. They said their good-byes, and she managed a thank-you for slaying the creep—no, the tubar—in the window.

Carter pushed against the door and locked it. Raising a hand, he muttered to himself, and she watched the air around the door glitter with symbols briefly.

"Another protection ward. Let's eat before these tacos get soggy," he told her and pulled her by the hand.

"Xander's a little…" She was unsure how to address the man in front of Carter.

Carter chuckled. "I hear he's quite the badass. He's also Peter's right-hand man and a damn good werewolf from what I've already seen. I'm glad he was here to keep you safe," he said and pulled her into his side before pressing his lips to her forehead.

After so much time away from him, it was sweet but not enough. Vanessa grabbed his face, and before she could second-guess herself, she kissed him. His mouth opened to hers without question. It was sweet, emotional, and left her aching for so much more.

Carter ended it and brushed his lips against hers one last time. "Food first and then I plan to do more of that," he said and waggled his eyebrows.

She chuckled as she pulled the bag out of his hand. Looking around, she realized the only counter space she had where they could eat was occupied. Carter seemed to notice her pause and closed his eyes.

He mumbled under his breath, and suddenly, he held a blanket. He laid it on the ground, lowered himself, and smiled up at her. "Picnic for two?"

"Wow, how did you do that?"

He waved his fingers dramatically. "Magic."

She shook her head and sat down.

"No, really. Serena taught me that and a few other things earlier tonight. I'm just excited it worked. It's the first time I've done it by myself." Carter beamed with both excitement and surprise as he reached into the bag and offered her a wrapped-up taco. "Now eat!"

They talked about their day between bites. She was surprised to hear him admit that his anxiety over her safety was making him unbearable at work. She, too, had been on edge between not knowing if danger was around the corner or if she simply missed him.

"My mom called me today," she said, dabbing at the corners of her mouth.

"Everything good?"

She nodded. "Yup. Mom and Dad decided to take a cruise for their anniversary, so she wanted to remind me they'd be gone."

Carter nodded. "You know, that's probably for the best. Hopefully by the time they return and I get to meet them, we will have this threat neutralized."

"I didn't think about it that way."

"Have you heard from Georgia?" he asked carefully.

Vanessa looked away. "No, she hasn't called."

Carter put their trash back in the bag and pulled her into the space between his legs. "Are you mad at her?"

Vanessa shrugged. "It wouldn't be fair to be mad at her for something she had no control over. I am a bit hurt over it all. I mean, that's a huge secret to keep from me, but again, it's not like she wanted to."

He kissed the top of her head. "I like her."

"She's the best, the sister I always wanted."

"Did I tell you she showed up at my house after our first date and ripped into me?" he asked, a smile teasing the corner of his mouth.

Vanessa twisted in his arms so she could look at him. "No! Tell me!"

Carter chuckled and wrapped his arms around her, then squeezed her to him. "She's a tough chick," he said before recounting the visit.

Vanessa laughed. "She never told me any of that, but I suppose she couldn't."

Carter kissed her temple before releasing her. "Why don't you get back to work, and I'll clean up our mess."

"I..." Her lips twisted, but she did not have a good argument.

A man who encouraged her and did not get upset she spent so much time on her craft was an anomaly. More often than not, she was praised for being a young business owner but reprimanded for not having more time to give her partner. Carter was unlike any of the others she had attempted dating.

"Thank you," she whispered before kissing him briefly. It was chaste and sweet. Her heart opened further for the man.

He gave her a light pat on the butt, sending her off to get to work, and she laughed. Being around Carter was easy. Silence did not agitate her nerves, and with everything out in the open, she felt as if they could breathe.

A few minutes later, she held her pliers in one hand and a headpin strung with a few chips of stone in the other.

Carter laid his hands on her shoulders and squeezed. "Why don't you just text her or call her?"

Tipping her head back, she met his gaze. "Huh?"

"Sweetheart, you've been sitting like that for ten minutes. You haven't moved, and a minute ago, I heard you mumble Georgia's name. Reach out to her."

She looked down at her hands. "Really? Ten minutes?"

Carter kissed her temple. "*Yes,* really."

Vanessa set down her tools and wiped her palms on her pants. Carter stepped away, giving her privacy, and settled on a comfortable chair he must have conjured.

She unlocked her phone and opened their last text, ignoring the slight tremble of her fingers.

Vanessa: Peter told me everything, as I'm sure you already know. I hope you know I'm not mad or upset. I could use a girl's night though. Love you!

The three little dots appeared instantly before disappearing and reappearing. This went on for nearly three minutes before Georgia's text vibrated Vanessa's phone.

Georgia: I'm so sorry I kept it from you. You're okay with everything?

Vanessa peered over at Carter, who was focused on the laptop before him. He looked like a college student rather than the doctor he was.

Vanessa: There's a lot to learn, but yes, we're okay!

chapter 20

Carter sat up straight, the satin sheet falling to his waist as droplets of sweat clung to his body. Glancing down, he stared at the impressive tent. Peering around his very empty room, he sighed before shifting sideways.

The cold floor pierced the bottoms of his feet as he lowered his elbows to his knees and cradled his head. His hair was damp with sweat, and his heart still thundered in his chest.

He did not know how many more sex dreams he could take involving Vanessa. Normally he *preferred* dreams of the X-rated variety, but his dick could not take more. Each dream was a reminder he had not made her entirely his.

He had not touched every delectable inch of skin on her body. He had not felt her inner muscles squeeze him dry. He had not completed their mate bond.

Shaking his head, he pushed to his feet and padded across the room. The cool morning air did nothing to soothe the ache he felt. Neither would the ice-cold shower he planned to take. Hell, he'd masturbated so many times, it was no wonder how his right arm was not stronger than his left.

It all became worse once he'd persuaded Vanessa to move into his guest bedroom. They argued and she hemmed and hawed before coming to the realization she was safer under his roof.

She was safer, but his mental state was near shattering.

His body constantly hummed at her nearness, and he was going through his days with a partial woody. There was not any relief in sight.

No, that was not true. He knew what the key was, but he did not know if it was worth the consequences. Consummating their soul mate bond would trigger their telepathic connection, like it had with his siblings, and it terrified him.

Carter did not have anything to hide from her. He was a rather open book since she had learned everything. But it did not change how he felt.

Giving one person an all-access pass to his most inner thoughts? Thoughts that did not always censor themselves? It was bad enough when a woman asked for an opinion, but if she peered into his head and saw his real thoughts of how she looked first thing in the morning? Or how a dress fit her? Or, shit... if she gained some weight? He would be fucked.

Not that some of those would matter. Vanessa was beautiful even when her hair was tousled from sleep, face was makeup-free, and her nipples greeted him through the thin fabric of her pajama top. She would still make his dick hard if she gained twenty pounds or lost them, although he was a real big fan of her current curves.

He was not sure about the possible arguments that could ensue from things he had not even spoken aloud. There wasn't anything more intimate than allowing someone into the deepest parts of your mind.

"Fine." He growled at his erection after a few minutes under the ice-cold water temp.

Placing one hand against the tile, he wrapped the other around his cock. In his mind, he recalled the taste of her rosy nipples, the taste of her tongue, the taste of her pussy, and the feel of her losing herself to the ecstasy his fingers and mouth gave her. In a matter of moments, his toes curled, and his body stiffened as his seed shot forth.

With his heart hammering at the force of his orgasm, he washed the mess before shutting off the water. His dick eased up some, deflating to a concealable size by the time he finished drying.

He took a step into his bedroom, then stopped short. Vanessa stood in his doorway, her eyes raking over his body as she licked her lips. The pressure in his balls increased, and his last masturbation session was all for naught.

"Sorry, the door was open..." she said, having to clear her throat.

Carter looked at the door and smirked. He knew for a fact it was shut. He had closed it the night before so he could jack off before sleeping. "Was it now?"

Her cheeks reddened and his dick twitched, knocking the towel loose from his waist. Vanessa gasped, her eyes darkening and her legs clamping shut at the very hard dick greeting her. He let her take in her fill before grabbing the towel from the floor.

It took every ounce of control not to storm over and pick her up before tossing her on his bed. He'd dreamed of her hair spilling over his pillow, her legs spread wide for him, and that pretty mouth running dry the moment he slammed his cock into her tight little pussy.

More blood flowed downward, and a pained groan slipped from his lips at the graphic images floating through his mind. It was another reason he was terrified of letting her into his mind. Sure, he liked taking his time during sex, but the fantasies she evoked within him were sure to scare the shit out of her.

Vanessa stepped forward, and he froze. He needed to ask her to leave, but his mouth went dry at the way she stalked toward him. Her pink tongue, sliding across her lower lip, mesmerized him.

She cleared her throat and audibly swallowed before lowering to her knees. "Let me help with… that."

He was helpless to her touch, rooted to the spot as her lips parted and took him in. Her soft hand wrapped around the base as she drew him to her mouth.

"Fuck..." He groaned, nearly coming on the spot with how turned on he was.

She moaned around her mouthful of dick, the vibration causing his knees to tremble. He needed to taste her. After indulging in another teasing suck, he forced himself free and smirked at her answering pout.

"I wasn't done!"

"Glad to hear that, but I need to fucking taste you, sweetheart," he said, pulling her to her feet and pushing down her pajamas to find her bare. "No panties?"

Vanessa shrugged, her cheeks reddening further. "I don't like to wear them under my pajamas."

He nodded and drew them to the bed, all the while telling himself they would not be having actual sex. "Come here so I can taste you while you suck my dick."

She bit the corner of her lip before grabbing the hem of her top and fully exposing her delectable body to his view. Carter stroked his length a few times at the view before waving her toward him.

He had no idea where he'd found the strength to hold back. His hips tried to pump forward and make her mouth his, but he wanted her to come all over his tongue before he found any sort of relief. Using his fingers, tongue, and mouth, he worked her. She was so fucking wet for him, her little nub swollen and eager for his attention.

If Carter died right then, he would die a happy man.

Vanessa's hips bucked faster, her muscles squeezing around his tongue. His heart raced, and his balls were heavy and tight. Carter needed to come with her. Carefully, he guided each thrust as he fucked her mouth and pussy.

His orgasm hit him hard and fast, and she followed. Their muffled groans filled the room, and she swallowed every drop he spilled. After a moment, he forced his fingers to release their grip, half-moons appearing on the flesh of her ass.

Vanessa dropped next to him on the bed. Her heavy breaths matched his own as he tried to regain any semblance of thought. The woman had left him numb in the most wonderful way. Running a hand down her leg, he licked his lips.

"Wow," she mumbled, her voice sleepy.

Carter turned on his side and kissed her calf. "Quite the start to our day," he muttered against her skin.

"Mhmm…"

His gaze landed on her full breasts and somehow his damn dick stirred, after the most explosive orgasm of his life. Carter ran a hand roughly down his face before lowering his feet to the floor. He listened to her shift behind him as he headed for his dresser.

"Great ass," she mumbled.

He slid a pair of black slacks up his legs and found her appreciative gaze on him. "Thanks," he said and grabbed her pajamas off the floor. "Here, we should probably get moving so I'm not late." Carter felt like the biggest asshole when a shadow of hurt and embarrassment crossed Vanessa's features.

"Right…" she said and slid her arms and head through the holes of her shirt.

He hurried to her side and took hold of her face. The right words escaped him, so he did the only thing he could. He captured her lips until she gasped for breath. Pressing his forehead to hers, he sighed. "No matter how badly I want to say fuck it and slam my cock into you…" He paused, smirking at the little gasp his words had evoked. "We both need to get to work."

"Okay." She breathed, and the puff of hair teased his lips.

Vanessa turned, not bothering to slip on her pajama bottoms, and he gave her round ass a swat. She jumped with a squeal, but the grin she offered over her shoulder reassured him she liked it.

He moved to his closet, looked down, and groaned. "Seriously, you need to calm the hell down," he snapped at his dick.

chapter 21

Vanessa could not stop smiling as the trees flew by. Carter's hand lay possessively on her jean-clad thigh as he drove her to her boutique. Her sex still hummed from the mind-blowing orgasm she had experienced at his hands.

When he retreated into the depths of his head, she felt a part of her heart crack. They had fooled around on his couch for the last week. Seeing his erection salute her that morning had made her feel sexy and bold.

She'd wanted to taste him for days, and the intimacy they shared that morning had been nothing short of amazing. Vanessa was surprised they still had not torn each other's clothes off and had sex.

Carter was proving to be the most gentlemen of men she had ever dated or met. He took care of her needs multiple times and, until that morning, he'd denied all of her offerings to make him feel better.

The car speakers cut out with the ringing of a call, drawing her back from the morning's activities.

"Hello," Carter said as they neared the boutique.

"Yo, we've got a little problem," a deep voice announced.

The energy in the car became stagnant, and they both stiffened at the man's words. Facing Carter, they shared a look before he returned his attention to the road. "What's going on?"

"I got here before y'all and noticed a new scent, so I followed it and noticed the back entrance was off. Someone broke in, man. I called the cops, and they're on their way since it seems like a *normal* crime."

All the blood drained from her face. Her mind whirled as she tried to recall if the insurance would cover everything. She tried remembering if she had locked up when Carter picked her up. His kisses along her neck had been distracting, but she doubted he would have let her forget to set the bolt.

"Pulling up now. I'll come up with Vanessa."

Carter did not bother waiting for the man's response and hit the End Call button on his steering wheel. He made the last turn, and the car jumped forward once he slipped into a parking spot. He squeezed her hand before releasing it so they could get out. At the front of the car, their hands linked again without a word as they moved toward the door where Joel stood.

Joel was taller and wider than Carter but smaller than Peter. His familiar face watched over her a few nights, but he had never spoken a word to her. "Peter's on his way," he said by way of greeting and offered

Carter a hand to shake. "I'm so sorry about this, Vanessa," he said, his eyes full of remorse.

"How bad is it?" she asked as Carter pulled her to his side after their handshake.

"I've seen a lot worse," he said and shrugged. "Your insurance should cover anything broken or stolen."

She sighed, not looking forward to the process ahead. A car's engine neared, and Carter turned them as a cop stepped out of an SUV. A thin man with dark hair and brown eyes approached them.

"Morning," he stated, taking in the three of them before his gaze landed on Joel. "I'm Officer Turnel. What seems to be the problem?"

Vanessa did not like the way the cop studied him. She slipped from Carter's embrace and moved to Joel's side, laying her head on his arm. "I asked Joel to meet us here, and he arrived first," she told the officer before turning her eyes up toward Joel. "Why don't you tell the nice officer everything you just told us?"

Carter's expression changed from hard and confused to amused as he took a moment to study his polished shoes.

Another car approached, and she wondered where everyone would park at the rate they were going. Instead of turning and finding Peter, they found another police car.

"Good morning, officer," Carter called.

The man took them in, his gaze going over them with a fine-tooth comb. "Morning," he muttered as he moved to Officer Turnel's side.

The officers looked from of them to the next as Joel recounted what he'd found. The cops nodded a few times before asking, "Who all has been in there?"

"We arrived only a few minutes before you," Carter said.

"I'm the only one who's stepped foot inside, but I didn't go past the counter, which is about three quarters the way in from the front door. In and out through the back door."

The second cop nodded. "Stay right here while we look things over."

Vanessa waited until they disappeared inside, then moved back to Carter's arms. The tension around him eased as he embraced her and pressed a quick kiss to her lips.

"What was that all about?" he asked, nodding toward Joel.

She looked toward the door and lowered her voice. "I didn't like the way he was looking at Joel, as if he was behind it."

Joel chuckled. "I can protect myself, but thanks."

"What the hell is their problem?" she asked, her brows pinching in thought.

"The cops around here aren't fans of us. It's like they sense something is different, but they chalk it up to us being on the wrong side of the law."

"Well that's not very fair!" Vanessa said.

The men shook their head, and Joel nodded toward Carter's car. Once they moved away from the open door, he narrowed his eyes. "Carter," he muttered low. "Something seem off to you too?"

"What's off to you?" Peter's voice boomed from their right, and all three of them startled. Peter paused at their reaction for a moment before joining them. "Sorry about your place, pipsqueak."

"Thanks," she said, offering him a small smile. "I still don't know what the damage is."

"Peter, there are two cops in there, and something is off," Joel stated in a lowered voice.

Peter looked them all over before his chin raised and his nostrils flared. He shrugged. "Smells human to me."

"Just wait until they come out," Carter replied. "Joel's not off about them. I kind of felt like a suspect and not the victim—"

"Hey!" Vanessa snapped. "My business."

Carter chuckled and pulled her back to his front. "Yes, sweetheart, it's your business."

"I see you two smoothed things over." Peter smirked before shaking his head with amusement.

"Not if he claims my business as his," she said and crossed her arms. Her words were harsh, but her tone was teasing.

Joel pulled the conversation back to the break-in and updated Peter on everything he had seen inside, starting from the strange scent he smelled.

For learning about the supernatural world recently, she was quite proud of herself for adjusting so well. She listened to them men speak quietly in case the officers stepped out. Still no one knew who the threat to her was, and she could tell that them not knowing was making them nervous.

Vanessa knew she should be worried, but she wasn't. She was not alone. She had Carter at her side, and at least one of Peter's wolves were assigned to her daily. If anything, she was annoyed to cause such problems for them. She was sure they all had better things to do other than babysit her.

Movement caught her eye when the two officers stepped out. They lowered their voices, so she could not hear their words, but by the way both Joel and Peter stiffened, she guessed they had.

"How bad is it?" she asked Officer Turnel before looking at the officer who had not introduced himself.

He shrugged. "As far as break-ins go? Not bad, but you'll want to file a claim to have all the glass counters replaced. You'll need to do inventory and report what is missing as well." His face turned, and a strange silence fell among them before he spoke again. "And who are you?" he asked Peter.

Peter uncrossed his arms and offered a big meaty hand. "Peter Rawley."

Another moment of silence passed. "How do you know Mrs.—"

"Miss Rayne, Vanessa Rayne," she said, since they had never bothered to ask. "He's a friend. Will you be able to find the culprit of this break-in?" she asked, before any more testosterone stepped into her business. With all the dicks flapping in the wind, it was a surprise she was not blind yet.

The no-name officer spoke. "We'll go through and see what evidence we can gather." The man shrugged. "I'm real sorry," he said, and she had the distinct impression he felt anything but sorry. She had no reason to disbelieve him. Plenty of people came off as assholes, but it did not mean they were outright malicious. But this man, like Joel had said... There was something about him.

"We'll write up a police report, and when you have a better idea of what is missing, you can come to the station to add it. We'll get you a copy so you can file your insurance claim," Officer Turnel said.

The cops walked to one of their cruisers, and after a few minutes of rummaging in the trunk, they passed the group on the way back inside. The four of them stood around for what felt like hours, waiting for them to be allowed in.

"Hey, it's Dr. Broderick. Look, there's been an emergency, and I don't think—"

Vanessa grabbed the phone from him and covered the microphone. "What are you doing? You're supposed to work at the hospital today, and those patients *need* you! I'll be fine."

Peter put a hand on Carter's shoulder. "We got her if you need to go in. Call any of us if you want to check in."

The tightness of his face told her he did not like it at all. Raising to her toes, she kissed him and smiled. "Go, Peter and Joel will stay with me."

He raised the phone to his ear. "Sorry, there was an emergency so I'm running late, but I'll be there in fifteen."

He hung up and sighed, his attention flitting to each of them. "I guess I'm going. I don't like it but… Thanks, guys, for keeping my girl safe," he said and shook each of their hands. When he turned to her, his eyes darkened with emotion before he grabbed her face and kissed her.

They watched him maneuver his car through the tight lot as she tried to unscramble her brain after his scorching kiss. Between Carter's insistence and whoever had taken over Ethan's body, she had been told she and Carter were soul mates multiple times. She refused to blindly accept it, but each time they touched, it was always the same.

Breathless, electrifying, and toe curling.

chapter 22

"Is Vanessa okay?" Brandy demanded through the phone.

Carter leaned his head against his office chair. "She wasn't there when it happened. Mind if I call you back in an hour or so? I'm only just finishing up at the hospital after running late this morning."

"Sure, Car. I'll talk to you later."

He had lost track of how many of those calls he'd received, and finally decided to set his phone to silent. His day had dragged after the break-in. He hated not being at her side and vowed to do everything possible to make sure it never happened again.

He was rather proud of himself for not reacting when she'd defiantly moved to Joel's side after the cop had stared at him judgingly.

A knock sounded on the door and he sighed. "Come in!"

"Hey, Doctor, the CT scans for room four thirty-five are in. Good job on playing catch-up, by the way. What happened?" Beverly asked.

He rolled the chair away from the desk. "Someone broke into my girlfriend's store," he said and pushed to his feet.

Her neck tightened, and her eyes widened. "Yeesh... That sucks. Let's get you to that last patient so you can get back to her."

After he finished, he thanked the nurses for having his back. He knew they took the brunt of the complaints for his lateness, emergency or not. Carter hurried to his car as he made another mental note to do something kind for them.

He pressed the call button on the steering wheel. "Call Vanessa Rayne."

"Calling Vanessa Rayne," the Bluetooth system called back.

His fingers curled around the steering wheel and released a few times before her voicemail picked up. He sighed and poked at his phone. The ringing filled his car again, and a deep voice answered, "Hey."

"Are y'all still at the store?"

"No. She didn't have a key to your place—which is bullshit, by the way—so I left Joel at the shop and brought her to her place," Peter said.

Carter winced. "Can I speak with her?"

Peter grunted, and Carter heard some shuffling.

"Who is it?" she asked Peter, her voice becoming louder. "Hello?"

"Hi, sweetheart, how are you holding up?" he asked, smiling at merely the sound of her voice.

"Carter?"

"Yeah, babe."

A silent moment passed before she cleared her throat. "Hi, I guess I'm okay. Trying to see what all I have so I can restock what was damaged."

"If there's anything I can help with, just tell me the word, okay?"

"Thanks, Carter," she said, her voice so soft he wondered if she was upset.

"Peter says you're at the apartment now," he said, preferring to imagine her in his home. "Pack up whatever you need and head back to the house. Use the office to set up your workspace. I'd wanted to give you the code earlier, but honestly I was afraid it would scare you off..." He turned left at the streetlight. "Can you memorize it, or do you need to write it down?"

"I-I'll remember it..." her raspy voice muttered.

His heart thundered in his chest as she called back the code and his instructions. Carter was rather surprised she had not fought him on the matter, as she was surrounded by her things. He was overwhelmed by how badly he wanted her to think of his home as theirs.

His heart did not have any concept of time. He'd found his mate, but taking the time to court her didn't seem to matter to it. Carter was torn between the need to claim her as his and the logical side of dating her.

"I need to make a stop before grabbing dinner and coming home. Are you in the mood for anything specific?" he asked, and images of going down on her came to mind. His dick twitched as it begged to slide back into her warm mouth.

"Surprise me," she said, and he wondered if her mind had also gone to the events that morning.

He adjusted himself as he slowed the car. "Be careful with what you ask for," he whispered. "See you soon."

"Bye," she said through a heavy breath, and he hoped her body ached like his did.

Carter peered down at the semi he was sporting. "Whoa, buddy, better stand down before Joel sees you."

Ten minutes later, he hit the lock button on the fob to his Audi and walked to the back door of Vanessa's shop. He raised his hand to knock, but Joel opened it before he could make contact.

"Hey."

"Hey," Joel said and stepped aside.

Carter's brows pinched together. "How'd you know—"

"Heard your car and smelled you the moment you stepped out of it," Joel said with a shrug.

Carter pursed his lips and nodded. "Nice. I forget how good your senses are compared to the rest of ours."

Joel chuckled. "We are superior," he teased.

All teasing vanished as Carter took in the boutique. Nearly every display was damaged, and items he had seen only days ago were gone.

"Did she say how much was taken?" Carter asked, jamming his hands into his pockets.

"Nah, but we helped her remove what was left. I've been cleaning up ever since," he said, nodding toward the full trash bags in the corner.

"Thanks, I really appreciate your help on this." He ran a hand over his jaw. "You didn't happen to catch anything since the cops don't seem to have much faith in finding the culprit, did you?"

"Whoever is behind this is human."

"Did she call her insurance?"

Joel nodded. "Yeah, she was on the phone for a bit with them before Peter got her out of here. He was pretty riled up with the state of things in here, so I told him I'd help clean up so she didn't have to. You've got a nice mate," he muttered, his words barely above a whisper.

"Have you found—" Carter said before thinking it was probably better not to ask about the man's mate.

"Have I found what? My mate?"

Carter raised a hand. "Sorry, I shouldn't have—"

Joel shook his head. "It's all right. No, I haven't met mine. A lot of us never do."

Carters brows pinched in confusion. "But if you don't... Doesn't that mean..." He tried to wrap his mind around the possibility.

Joel shrugged. "Yeah, no sex... It will also shorten my lifespan if I don't meet my mate."

Not wanting to bring the man any more pain, Carter nodded toward a glassless display. "Help me carry this out to the back?"

With Joel's help, they cleared out the broken items, then he made a few calls—including Serena, who pointed him to a wholesale supplier he could order from over the phone. New reinforced doors were put in. He took a risk and picked new display cases, but he wanted to take care of her. She did not need to worry about her store on top of the fact some demon or other thing was looking for her. It took a bit of a miracle, but her new things would arrive by the next day. After some finagling with the alarm company he used, he was also able to set up the install for the following day.

He hoped she did not fight him, because he could not help the urge to keep her safe and make things better.

Joel nodded slowly. "I'm impressed. I'll get some of the guys here in the morning, and we'll help move the new stuff in."

Carter grinned, proud of himself for the feat. "Thanks, man. Honestly, thanks for everything. I could not have cleaned this out by myself, and you had most of it done. I'm willing to pay you guys for the—"

Joel raised a hand, and his face no longer held the easy-going expression from before. "Don't insult us. This is the right thing to do, and we like helping. Plus, we both know you'd have called in reinforcements."

He chuckled at the thought of all his brothers swinging in to help. "Thanks, man." Carter twisted his wrist and stared at the time with wide eyes. "Well, shit, I think it's time we get going."

chapter 23

Vanessa rolled her neck before pushing to her feet and stretching. She had been sitting for hours, crafting new items to replace the ones some scumbag had taken. Normally she found the process relaxing and liberating, but not today.

She turned toward the large man taking up most of Carter's couch. "Why again are you babysitting me?" she asked and moved to the fridge.

"I'm not getting paid, so I'm definitely not a babysitter," Peter called without bothering to look at her.

"Whatever... Look, I'm fine here. Carter told me how to use the alarm, and only his family and your pack know I'm here," she told him as she poured a glass of water.

"My pack doesn't know. Only a few of us do. Now will you shush? I need to hear this," he said, leaning toward the TV.

She laughed. "I never would have guessed you liked soap operas."

Peter shushed her and focused on the man and woman arguing on the screen.

Vanessa carried her glass to the table and tucked one leg under her bottom as she sat. She checked her phone for any messages first but found none. There was nothing from Carter, and she mentally chided herself for being disappointed.

He scared the crap out of her when he got home after eight with their food. By then, Peter had left a wolf to watch the house because something important had come up with his pack. In the morning, she found a note from Carter in the kitchen, letting her know he went in early but that he would check in later.

She was not sure if he was avoiding her, or if there really were things he needed to do. The morning of the break-in, she nearly had to push him into his car and make him go to work. Now she felt as if he'd brushed off the incident and left her in the care of the pack alpha.

One minute, she was his mate and they were exploring the connection between them, and the next, trouble found her and he was nowhere to be seen.

She shook off her morose mood and set her phone to Do Not Disturb. If he did not want to contact her, that was fine. They had only fooled around some, and it did not make him her anything. At the reminder of his mouth on her body, a bolt of need shot down between her legs.

"Just because he gives good tongue, doesn't mean he's a good match," she muttered to herself.

A groan from the couch made her hands still.

"Pipsqueak, please keep your thoughts to yourself."

She narrowed her gaze on the back of Peter's head. "What are you talking about?" she asked, her cheeks flaming. She debated the possibility he had heard her softly spoken words over the sound of his show.

Peter tapped his left ear. "Werewolf hearing."

She covered her face and groaned. "You heard that?"

"Mhmm… And whatever has you second-guessing Carter, you should probably let it go. He had a few things to do before seeing his patients."

Her embarrassment vanished as frustration replaced it. "Mind your own damn business."

Peter chuckled. "I was, before you decided to share with the class that Carter gives 'good tongue,'" he said, his fingers curling into air quotes.

"Ugh!" she snapped and grabbed a bead and wire. "You can get your own food at this rate."

His deep laughter boomed, the sound filling the open room. "I never asked you to make me lunch, Pipsqueak."

The man was infuriating. Instead of feeding the conversation, she lowered her head and returned to work. At least one good thing had come out of the entire situation. Inspiration struck and she got to work on a few new pieces.

A couple of hours later, a phone rang. She peered at her own, but it lay still with the screen black.

"Hey!" Peter said and chuckled after a few moments. "Well, I'm not surprised. She's been in a bit of a mood."

"Hey!" Vanessa called.

Peter tilted his head in her direction, and she could see the smirk on his lips before he spoke to the caller. "Yeah, I'll let her know... That works. I'll see you in thirty."

"Who was that?" she called as he lowered the phone.

"Carter. I guess he's been trying to get a hold of you," he said around a loud yawn.

She grabbed her cell phone and remembered she had set it to Do Not Disturb. She had missed three calls and five text messages from him, but no voicemails had been left. When she opened the messages, she noted he'd checked in a few times before asking her to have Peter bring her to the boutique. Carter even apologized for not being able to check in sooner, as a few patients had had emergencies. Her frustration from before deflated as she was reminded of how important he was to his patients.

"Yo! Pipsqueak?" Peter called, clearly not for the first time.

She blinked a few times and met his gaze for the first time since lunch. "Sorry?"

"I said, if you want to change, go do it now because I have to drop you off."

She nodded. "Yeah, that would be great. Go back to your show, and I'll be ready soon."

Peter's attention returned to the TV as she collected her finished pieces. Vanessa tidied the dining room table but left her supplies with the intention of returning to them when they came home. She paused briefly and shot Peter a glance before she corrected herself mentally.

Carter's home. Not their home.

Rushing to the room she slept in, she decided she was in need of a hot shower before they left. Her muscles were tight from hours at the table, and the heat would soothe the ache. She took an extra five minutes to let the water pound into her muscles before shutting it off.

Vanessa made quick work of drying off and slipped into a pair of skinny jeans and a red tank top that did everything for her breasts. She was not wearing it for Carter. No, she just needed a little picker upper after the last forty-eight hours.

"Shut up," she muttered at the mirror as she dove into her makeup bag. She retrieved the mascara, slid the wand over her lashes, and applied lipstick. Then she ran her fingers through her hair and nodded with satisfaction. "There."

"Pipsqueak! If you're done chatting with yourself, do you think we can move along?" Peter yelled.

"Bastard..." she grumbled and shook her head at the sound of his laughter.

She grabbed her clutch and keys and glared at Peter. "I get you have awesome supernatural hearing, but can you be a gentleman and pretend you don't hear everything that comes out of my mouth?"

"No. Leave the keys."

"No? Wait, what? I need them to get into my shop," she said, her head cocking to the side.

Peter shook his head and grabbed her by the elbow. "Your key won't work. To secure the shop, we changed out the door and locks."

Her mind switched gears when he stopped her in front of Carter's alarm panel. She set it, and they hurried out to his car. Peter helped her into her seat and closed the door behind her.

"The shop's door was changed?" she asked as she faced Peter.

"Mhmm..." he replied as he put one arm behind her seat to back into the street.

Her brows pinched in thought. "I think that violates my leasing agreement. Crap, what am I going to do now? Maybe Mrs. Ruby will understand the situation and not be upset," she muttered.

Peter chuckled. "Do you always do that?"

"Huh?"

"Do you always talk to yourself?"

She pursed her lips in thought. "Yeah, I guess so. I'm an only kid, so Mom and Dad weren't always around to chat. I guess it's how I work some things out."

"Makes sense."

"I should probably call my landlady, right?"

Peter put a hand over her unlocked phone. "How about you wait until later to do that?"

Vanessa did not know what good it would do to wait, but there was no reason not to. The time would help her come up with an argument for why the door had been replaced without prior approval.

When they arrived at the small parking lot behind the building, Peter met her at the front of the car and guided her by the elbow to the much more sophisticated door. There was a regular lock, but just above it was a keypad—another number for her to memorize. It was no wonder they did not just fall out of her head with the hundreds of passwords rattling around.

Peter pounded on the door, and her eyes widened at the solid sound. A moment later, Joel greeted them with a grin. "Welcome!"

She giggled at the large man and shook her head in amusement. Before she could say anything, Carter appeared, and all her thoughts seemed to fall out with the numbers and passwords.

"Hi, sweetheart, can you turn around for me?"

The air around her became thick, but she did as he asked without a word.

"We have a little surprise for you," he said, and his fingers brushed her face as a blindfold covered her eyes.

She heard some shuffling, her other senses amplified with her sight removed. "What's going on? Why do I smell paint?"

He cupped her cheeks. "Trust me," he whispered and pressed his lips to hers. They were soft and full, and she kissed him back without thought. Somewhere inside she knew she should be annoyed with him, but in that moment, all she could think about was tasting his lips.

The kiss ended faster than she would have liked, and he moved around her. "I've missed you," he whispered and brushed his lips over the skin at her neck. A little shiver ran down her body, and her sex flooded with desire.

He was both bad and good for her. She had never reacted so strongly to a man, but on the other hand, *everything* with him was too strong, too fast, and too needy.

Before her thoughts could become darker, he guided her forward. She had been in her shop hundreds of times, so when he approached where the counter was, she stopped. Carter chuckled and urged her further, her brows pinching in confusion.

"I didn't want you to lose too much business after the break-in, so with everyone's help, you can open tomorrow," Carter said and pulled off the blindfold.

The afternoon sunlight made her blink a few times. Once her eyes focused, she slowly spun in a circle. She raised a hand to her mouth as she took it all in. New display cases, better than her last ones, filled the shop, and her counter had been shifted.

"With Serena's help, I picked out some display cases to replace the broken ones. I've added a security system to help prevent any future problems, and with my sister's and Serena's business insight, we made a few interior design changes which will hopefully help business."

Vanessa noted the subtle cameras, two pointing toward the back and front doors, one on the register, and two more at angles to catch everything else. The paint on the walls was changed from white to a blue-green, which reminded her of the ocean. Fun modern light fixtures that had to have cost a fortune lit the space in the most beautiful way.

Vanessa envisioned her bank account, and everything became blurry with unshed tears. "I don't know if I can pay you back."

Carter grabbed her hands and squeezed. "There's nothing to pay back. This is our gift to you."

She ignored him. "This is too much... How in the world did you guys do all of this in one day?"

"A lot of us chipped in our time," Joel said, a huge grin filling his face.

Vanessa let go of Carter's hand and embraced the bear of a man. "Thank you," she said into his large chest. Pulling back, she turned toward Peter. "You knew all about this, didn't you?"

Peter shrugged, his lips twitching. "It was Carter's doing. We just helped."

"Do you like it?" Carter asked.

She turned to face him, and she found worry lines marring his forehead and his eyes filled with anxiety. Vanessa took her new shop in one more time and grinned. "I love it! It's honestly what I dreamed of and planned on working toward but I couldn't afford. Please, let me repay you…"

Carter shook his head and moved forward to tip her chin up. Their eyes met and held before he spoke. "I've been waiting for you to enter my life, and I'm going to do everything humanly possible to take care of you."

chapter 24

The rest of their week went off without a hitch. Vanessa had fought him a few different times about wanting to pay him back, but each time, he resorted to kissing her senseless. It was not a bad solution to the increasingly annoying argument. Her little whimpers told him without words that she was not complaining over his tactics either.

Each morning, they woke in separate beds and got ready for the day. They met in the kitchen and enjoyed light conversation as they drank their coffee and ate breakfast. One of Peter's men was always near, watching Carter's home for any danger lurking nearby.

Thankfully, nothing had happened, but that also meant they were no closer to discovering who was supposedly on her trail. And the cops still had no leads on who had broken into her shop.

Every day, a piece of his heart broke off and became claimed by Vanessa. She was an easy woman to love, not that he was there yet. She was sweet, funny, kind, and witty. They worked together in the kitchen a few nights too. Carter taught and fed her some family-favorite meals his father had shown him how to cook, and Vanessa treated him to some delicious desserts she could bake thanks to her grandmother.

The only place in their relationship where nothing progressed was with sex. The blame fell on him. He kissed her and pleased her in other ways when they fooled around, but he still feared what would happen when they bonded. The coward he was, he had not even told her.

Instead, each confused and hurt expression she threw his way—when he stopped things from getting too heavy—sliced him through the heart. And he let them. He deserved to be beaten for making her feel unwanted.

It was not that Carter did not want her. He just could not set his fears aside. Vanessa was his soul mate, yet he could not bring himself to lay claim. She deserved better than him.

Her thighs clamped around his head. "Oh my God!" she cried, and he worked his tongue and fingers at a clipped pace. Her back bowed off the couch again, and her legs fell away.

Carter removed his fingers and licked them clean, savoring her taste. Her chest rose and fell, and he could not stop the smug grin on his face. Her hair was a beautiful mess on the couch and a sheen of sweat made her body glow in her post-orgasm haze.

He shifted to behind her, then pulled her back to his bare chest and smiled when her ass scooted toward his raging erection. He ran a hand over her hip as he put his nose to her neck and breathed her in.

"I should be concerned over the fact you won't let me take care of this," she said and rolled her hips, teasing his straining dick. "But I'm too spent…"

He smiled against her hair. What she said was exactly his plan. Each night they would fool around, and he made sure to give her enough orgasms to exhaust her.

With the TV's soft glow on her, he ran his fingertips along her smooth skin. Carter explored her soft belly, then they traveled up her ribs to the plump flesh of her breasts until the pad of his thumb teased her nipple.

Vanessa swatted at his hand. "Mmm… no more. If I come again, I think you'll break my vagina."

He chuckled, and his hips moved forward without thought. "I'm pretty sure it's not my fingers and mouth that want to break your pussy."

Vanessa sucked in a harsh breath and moaned at his words. He realized his mistake before she sat up. "See… When you say shit like that but stop us every time from having sex, it sends mixed messages."

Carter clenched his jaw. She was right and he was an asshole for doing it, especially for doing it to her. The magical thread tying them was one thing, but with each passing day, he fell deeper.

"Yeah, great. More fucking silence!" Vanessa snapped, waving her hands around before she pushed to her feet. She crossed her arms over her body, standing naked yet shielding herself from him.

"Sweetheart," he said as he sat up.

Vanessa squatted to pick up her panties and waved one finger in his direction. "No, don't fucking sweetheart me!"

He opened his mouth and closed it as she shimmied the scrap of fabric up her thighs and into place. Carter stood and took a step toward her, but she put out her hand.

Vanessa grabbed her night shirt from the couch's armrest. "No. Please don't touch me. All you're going to do is make this more confusing, and I just can't handle it right now."

His shoulders slumped. He wanted to comfort her but respected her need for space, even if it sucked. "Okay," he said and ran a hand down his face. "My intention is not for you to feel—"

"I'd say used, but oh wait, all you've done is give me a ton of orgasms. Thanks, by the way," she called over her shoulder as she paced the space in front of the TV.

He should not find her sexy as hell as she paced the floor, her anger directed at him, but he did. He always knew he needed a strong, smart-mouthed woman in his life. The mild-tempered ones had been fine when he needed to get off, but they would never satisfy him in the long haul.

Vanessa was not afraid to tell him what she liked or if he had pissed her off.

She froze, her eyes glued to the news playing quietly in the background. "What did they just say?"

"I don't know. What's wrong?" Carter asked and grabbed the controller to his DVR and rewound the clip.

"We've just learned the body found early this morning at the Mandolin Apartments belongs to Tyler Babcock. The police are asking the public for any information that will help solve his murder."

She gasped. "Tyler's dead?"

It took Carter a second for his brain to catch on. "Tyler? Your neighbor Tyler?"

Vanessa faced him, her eyes wide with shock and tears brimming. Her mouth opened and closed a few times, and he could not sit back any longer. He pushed to his feet and rushed to her. He pulled her into his arms and held her tightly as the first sob escaped.

"Oh my God, who would kill Tyler?" she mumbled into his chest, her hot breath against his skin as her fingers dug into him.

He did not know what to say. Carter kissed her hair and lay his cheek on the top of her head. "I don't know, sweetheart, I don't know..."

His mind flipped through varying scenarios, starting with the first and only time he had seen Tyler: nearly dead from lycan venom poisoning him with each passing second. It was clear to Carter the man had been a witch, but Carter knew nothing else about him except where he'd lived.

Had Tyler attracted more attention? Had he been killed in an attempt to get to Vanessa? Was his murder completely coincidental?

Carter did not have answers. All he could do was hold Vanessa in his arms, their argument tabled for the time being as she grieved the man's passing.

Vanessa swayed in his arms, exhaustion from her orgasms combining with her crying. Carter shut off the TV and scooped her into his arms. He maneuvered through the darkened living room, only the moonlight streaming through to guide him as his eyes adjusted.

"What if they'd broken into my apartment instead?" she whispered.

"But they didn't," he said. "And now you're here with me. There isn't anything I wouldn't do to keep you safe." Vanessa meant too much to him to allow a single hair on her head to be hurt. Once Vanessa realized they had his family and their magical arsenal at their disposal she wouldn't feel so overwhelmed.

"I don't want to be alone tonight..." she said against his chest, her voice whisper-soft. "Hold me. This once, will you please hold me?"

His knees threatened to buckle at her words. Never had a woman's innocent request affected him. "I'll hold you for as long as you let me," he muttered against her forehead. Retracing a few of his steps, he decided that if he were going to hold her, it would be in his bed.

Carter set her on her feet before pulling the covers back. Vanessa crawled into the center of his bed and turned on her side, facing away from him. He dropped his jeans, leaving on only his underwear, and slipped in behind her. Pulling her flush against him, he placed his hand over hers and their fingers interlaced.

Needing to comfort her, he kissed the spot where her T-shirt exposed her neck. "I'm so sorry," he stated before hugging her tightly.

"So am I..."

He held her to him, listening to her breaths until they became shallow when sleep came, and only then did he follow. They barely moved all night. When one of them shifted, the other followed, always seeking out the other's touch or embrace.

Carter woke first and found himself on his back. Vanessa's leg lay across his as she hugged the side of him. One hand rested over his heart, and her face was soft with sleep. The sheet had made its way down their bodies, and his morning wood was barely concealed in his underwear, the tip peeking out of the elastic band.

He had never slept with a woman in a bed and not had sex. The very intimate act tugged at his heart, and he knew his resolve was waning. He would not be able to hold back much longer, but he refused to claim her without her knowing the consequences.

Each time he avoided her advances for more, rejection flashed hot in her eyes. He could not continue this way, especially not after the beginning of last night's argument.

His fingers found her hair and brushed it off her face. The silky strands fell forward again without weight to keep them in place. Vanessa's breathing changed, and he stilled.

A little moan slipped from her lips, so he waited to see if she would wake. It was still early enough that she could sleep, and he did not want to wake her—not to the reminder of Tyler's murder or the pain Carter inflicted.

A moment passed as she stirred, then her body stiffened. Looking down, he saw her eyes wide as they took in his dark room. "It's early. Go back to bed, sweetheart."

Her head came up slowly, and their gaze met. "Am I in your bed?" she asked, her voice groggy with sleep.

The raspy sound sent a shiver down his skin. "Yeah," he managed to say past a lump of desire.

He watched her and noted the moment everything flooded back to her. Vanessa sat up, taking the sheet with her. It fell at her waist and exposed him to the thighs. Carter tucked a hand under his head, afraid to do much more and upset her.

"Oh my God," she whispered, and her gaze met his again. "Tyler's dead?"

He dipped his chin in response.

Vanessa brought her knees to her chest and shoved her fingers into her hair. "Who could have killed him?"

"Not sure, sweetheart, but…"

She twisted her body, her knees dropping against his thigh and one hand bracing her weight. "But what?"

Carter lay his hand between her knees, and his thumb caressed the smooth skin. "Tyler was a witch."

Little lines formed between Vanessa's brows. "He was a witch? How do you know that? How did you figure that out? Wait... Were you ever going to tell me?" She asked question after question, her anger visibly rising.

Carter held back the smirk threatening to break free. He did not want her upset with him but preferred seeing the fire in her eyes to the anguish from moments before. "He was. I sensed his wards around his apartment door the first time I went to your place, and honestly, I don't know. It wasn't really my place to tell you his business."

"So why are you telling me now?" she snapped.

"If a lycan bit him previously and now he's found murdered, I'm going to take a stab in the dark and say whoever killed him wasn't a human."

Her lips parted with understanding. "Oh..."

"Worst-case scenario?"

"Yeah?" she asked.

He braced his weight on his elbow to get closer to her. Carter breathed her in and sighed. "Worst case, whoever killed him was really looking for you..."

She shook her head. "I was afraid you'd say that."

Carter raised his free hand and cupped her cheek. Vanessa nestled into his palm, and her eyes closed for a second before her hard eyes met his, and she pulled back. "What are we doing, Carter?"

He rubbed his lips together to stave off the need to take her mouth with his. His heart thundered. He was unsure how to answer her question.

A little growl escaped her lips, and she tossed both hands in the air. "I can't do this," she said and turned her body away from him.

The sudden movement snapped him out of it. He wrapped an arm around her waist and pulled her back and under him. Her wide eyes looked up at him, with her hair fanned across his pillow, her chest rising and falling, and her hard nipples visible through her night shirt.

Carter lowered himself between her legs and pinned her to the bed, ignoring the fact she would feel his hardness in the position. He ran a thumb across her lower lip, wishing he could suck on it but knowing he could not prolong the conversation any longer.

"I'm sorry if I've made you feel rejected, sweetheart. That was never my intention," he said.

She huffed, and pain shone in the depths of her eyes. "Well, you failed miserably then."

Carter dropped his head. "God, I'm so sorry." When she did not give him a response, he met her gaze. "There are things about my family you don't understand—"

"Because you've never tried to explain them," she said stubbornly. "You know, for someone who keeps insisting we're soul mates, you sure don't trust me with shit."

Her words sliced through him. He could not argue with her on the matter either. It was never that he did not trust *her*. He just never trusted the soul mate thing, even after watching his siblings find theirs.

"When Brandy met Ryan, it was one thing to wrap my head around the fact we were witches. I did not understand or believe they were soul mates. Chemistry? Hell yeah. As a medical professional, I understand the power of pheromones, but soul mates? No. Then Ethan and Serena got together, and it was just as fast and just as deep. I could not help but wonder if there was something in the water making them crazy. When Max found Claudia injured, I tried helping, but at my initial approach, he tossed me across the room—me, his brother, for a woman he'd only just met. That was the moment I realized there was something science could not explain away."

When his vision went hazy at the memory, Vanessa cupped his cheek and forced him to look at her. "Some things can't be explained."

He studied her a moment. There in his darkened room, with their bodies pressed together—skin touching—he truly understood Max's reaction. It was a miracle he had not been more aggressive around Peter or Joel.

"There's more..." he stated, finally ready to lay it all out.

There was no way he could walk away from her, but she had a right to know. If she did not accept all of him, he would lead a lonely life. No other woman would be right for him, not now—not after he'd met his mate.

"When each sibling found their destined mate, it was clear that the moment they had sex, they cemented their bond as soul mates. A telepathic link formed between them, and that's what has held me back. I want you on a level I've never experienced. You're my breath, my every thought, my forever, and I've had a hard time wrapping my head around it all. There was no way I could allow us to bond without you knowing the truth. The idea of connecting on a telepathic level used to scare the shit out of me."

The words had tumbled out of him, and with the full truth out, a weight was removed from his shoulders. After letting the words loose, he realized how stupid he had been acting all along.

chapter 25

"Telepathic?" she muttered, her hand dropping to her side.

Carter nodded, his lips twisting to the side. "Yeah, telepathic. Crazy, right?"

Her eyes rounded as she took a few seconds to let his truth sink in. She had lived her entire life with very few people to share her thoughts with. Now Carter was informing her that once they had sex, he would be privy to her deepest thoughts?

"Wait? How does it work? Like, are we talking we can communicate telepathically, or you're going to know I secretly hated Georgia for six months when she dated my crush?"

Carter opened his mouth and closed it. "You hated your best friend?"

She waved away his silly question. "That's not the point. Let's get back to this *if we have sex, we'll become telepathic* thing."

He sat up and she missed the weight of his body immediately. He was like one of those anxiety blankets. The moment he lay on her, she felt everything would be okay. Vanessa sighed and also brought herself to a sitting position, tucking her legs cross-legged underneath her.

Carter ran a hand down his face. "I don't know. I've never actually asked how it works. When Ryan got kidnapped last year—"

"Whoa! Your brother-in-law got kidnapped? By who?"

Carter chuckled. "He did, and by some crazy demon trying to get to Brandy. Anyhow, when that went down, she was able to use their link and learn he was okay and where to find him."

"So that sounds like she had to make the connection," she said. "What about Serena and your brother?"

He snuck a peek at her from the corner of his eyes. "Well," he said, then cleared his throat. "When Serena was kidnapped—"

Vanessa put a hand on his arm, stopping him. "Whoa, wait a minute. Serena was *also* kidnapped? Let me guess, another demon?"

Carter smirked, and her heart squeezed in the sweetest way. "She was, but no, not a demon. A witch posing as one."

"Of course, why didn't I think of that…"

"As I was saying, when Serena was kidnapped, Ethan was able to communicate with her and also figure out her whereabouts."

"So, if we link up, it will pretty much be useful in the likely scenario one of us pisses off the wrong person and we get kidnapped. Wonderful." Sarcasm dripped from her words, and she scrubbed her face. "Do you know anything else about it other than it's useful in captivity?"

"Not really. Honestly, the idea of someone getting into my thoughts freaked me out, so I repressed that wee bit of information until you came along," he said, a boyish smile tugging at his lips.

"Well, I appreciate you not forcing your thoughts on me without my consent. Ha! Who would have thought consent to a telepathic link should be included with consent to intercourse?" she joked, her mind reeling at all the possibilities a link could bring.

Carter twisted, and she tried to keep her focus on his face and not the hard planes of his chest and abs. He looked better than any of her wet dreams, but she needed time to think things through.

He pinched her chin and forced her eyes to his. "I care about you more than I have any other woman. It's absurd, considering how little time we've known each other. I may not be able to explain what's brought us together, and I can admit it used to terrify me, but I don't want to lose you. If you decide all of this is too much, I'll respect your decision. But know this now, I won't walk away until I know you are safe."

Her immediate response was to tell him she wanted him. All of him. Crazy magic, telepathic link, family who tended to get kidnapped... All of it. But she didn't. She stared at him and nodded in understanding. "I need time to process," she said instead, logic winning the current round.

Carter closed the gap between them and brushed his lips against hers. It was soft and sweet and packed an emotional punch that left her mind spinning. He held the power to ruin her, and she hated it. She had never given any man an ounce of that power, but with Carter, it was natural.

He was the first thing she thought about in her day and the last before sleep took over. They would need to interview his siblings to understand the bond better, but she knew deep inside she was in it for the long haul. Her mind would put up a fight, but something told her they were one kiss from opening the flood gates to her deepest thoughts.

Carter stood and offered her a hand. "We should start getting ready."

Glancing at the clock on the nightstand, she realized more time than she'd expected had passed with their one-on-one. She accepted his help and stood before him. "Thank you."

He chuckled. "I mean, I know you can get out of bed yourself, but I was just making it a bit easier."

She smirked and shook her head. "No, I mean thank you for being honest with me. Thank you for telling me everything. I understand why you've been so wishy-washy with me."

He laid a hand where her neck and shoulder met, the familiar zing moving along her skin at his touch. "I'm sorry I hurt you with waiting so long. I—" he stopped and cleared his throat. "I could never hurt you on purpose, I hope you know that."

They say the eyes are the window to the soul, and she finally understood the phrase. In that moment, she stared into his. Raw emotion laid out for all to see. "I know that now." She grabbed his wrist and gave it a squeeze. "No more half-truths, okay?"

Carter agreed, and they sealed it with an innocent kiss before she padded out of his room to hers.

Vanessa brushed her teeth, did her hair, and dressed, her mind in a fog all the while. She processed everything they had talked about that morning. By the time she walked into the kitchen, she was no closer to wrapping her mind around a morsel of what she'd learned.

Carter leaned against the counter as he sipped his coffee with one hand and held his phone with the other. He wore a white button-down, long-sleeve dress shirt and gray slacks, which fit perfectly on his narrow waist.

Vanessa went to his side and smiled at her own mug. Every morning since he'd learned how she took her coffee, she found it hot and ready for her.

"Okay, I'll give Peter a try in case he caught wind of something the cops haven't. Thanks again, Junior. Give Debbie my love," Carter said before ending the call. He slid the phone into his pocket and smiled at her. "You look beautiful."

Vanessa grinned. "Thanks, you look pretty handsome yourself."

"Thanks."

"Was that your brother?" she asked. Trying to recall every one of his siblings was getting easier the longer she was around him.

Carter drank deeply before nodding. "It was. He's a private investigator and used to be a cop. I called to see if he heard anything about Tyler's murder."

"And?"

He pursed his lips. "He hasn't, but he said he'll ask around. Junior suggested asking Peter since I mentioned Tyler was a witch."

"So, not to be rude, because Peter has been seriously great—albeit annoying— but if he's a werewolf, why would he know witch stuff? I mean, wouldn't it be separate people's business?" she asked, trying to understand the structure.

"Peter's the pack alpha. He tends to know all supernatural business, or seems to try. He can't protect his people if he has his head in the sand about the others."

She nodded. "That actually makes a lot of sense." Vanessa took another sip of her coffee and set it down on the counter. "Will you call him now?" she asked as she wrapped her arms around his waist and leaned into his hardness.

Carter raised a brow. "I can... Sweetheart?"

"Hmm?"

"You're taking everything I said earlier pretty well... I kind of expected you to want space from me."

Her lips pulled into a tight line as she nodded. "I'm still processing, but I like being in your arms," she admitted and pressed her cheek to his chest.

Carter wrapped an arm around her. "Not complaining at all." He slid out his phone, and she watched him pull up his recent calls before pressing on Peter's name. "Hey... No, she's fine." Carter kissed the top of her head, and she sighed with pleasure at the sweetness.

Closing her eyes, she listened to Carter's voice rumble in his chest as he brought up Tyler. The sounds wrapped around her in a blanket of warmth and comfort. She never felt that from simply holding another human.

"Yeah, a few weeks ago, he'd been bitten by a lycan, and I healed him enough so he wouldn't die. I just don't know if his murder had anything to do with Vanessa or if it was random, you know?" Carter said. "All right, thanks. We appreciate it."

"So?" she asked, tipping her head back when he ended the call.

"He heard about the murder but didn't realize Tyler was a witch. Peter says he'll send someone to look into it."

chapter 26

They had nothing.

No, that was not true. They had been able to determine Tyler's death was related to the supernatural. No one knew who was behind it though, because it was covered up well. The person interested in Vanessa was still unknown to them too. The longer they remained shrouded in darkness, the more Carter worried. What were they waiting for? Had they changed their mind about Vanessa?

His family had already experienced two kidnappings, and while Claudia and Max had not been kidnapped themselves, technically a kidnapping situation was how they'd found her. She had been fleeing from her captor, with her child in tow.

Carter shook his head. Statistically speaking, for one family to have that many abductions was unheard of. He could not deny it as a possibility. What he worried most about if it did happen, was that Vanessa was a human and could not protect herself.

A week had passed since he told her the entire truth. He had finally come to terms with it, and deep dark thoughts be damned, he was ready to cement their connection. On the other hand, she had not brought it up again. Their physical intimacy had reverted to first base, and while his dick was supremely pissed off about that, he could not rush it.

Everyone was busy. Between their own lives and helping them search into who was a threat to Vanessa, they were not able to ask for more on the telepathic bond. But he planned on doing it soon at their family dinner.

Vanessa walked into the living room with her phone to her ear, her head tipped back with laughter. "Stop it. That did not happen!"

He fucking loved her.

The truth hit him out of nowhere. No, that was not true. It had crept up on him with each passing day, but in that moment, he realized he was done for.

Her smile, her laugh, her kindness... The woman was patient and intelligent, and he was head over heels in love with her. He even loved the way she softly snored.

He pushed to his feet, his heart hammering in his chest. Carter needed air. He forced a smile for her benefit and pulled open the door to the patio. The summer heat was in full swing, and it slapped him in the face. Sucking in a lungful of air, he tried not to hyperventilate at his realization.

"Holy shit, I fucking love her," he mumbled and shut his eyes, taking in the warm rays of sunshine on his face. "I love her…"

As it settled in his mind and heart, his chest rumbled with laughter. Joy burst forth, consuming him at the beautiful feeling he felt for a human who was not family.

Love.

"Are you okay?" Vanessa asked, causing him to jump. She eyed him cautiously, the phone no longer to her ear.

He grinned, even as fear tried to affect his mood. "I'm great. Just uh… wanted some fresh air." What would he do if she decided she would not accept him?

Carter pushed aside the negative thoughts finding their way in. He jogged to her side and picked her up in his arms and spun them. Vanessa's squeal of delight stung his ear, but it never dampened his grin.

"How's Georgia?" he asked, directing her attention from his odd behavior.

They stopped spinning, and when he did not release her, Vanessa wrapped her arms around his waist. "She's good. Just got back into town and was telling me some crazy story about an elderly couple screwing in the woods."

Carter paused before bursting into laughter. "Well, good for them."

"Right? I hope we're doing it when we're old." Her eyes rounded when she realized what she'd said.

"Thinking about us growing old together?" he asked, excited at the thought.

She shrugged before chewing on her lip. "Maybe."

Carter stared at her mouth as blood rushed south. His hands moved and grabbed her ass. "Maybe?"

Vanessa's moan set his body on fire. Needing a taste, he crushed his mouth to hers. His thick length pulsed as he drew her impossibly close. Her hands slid up his chest before she cupped his face.

"Carter." She gasped before devouring him.

Their kiss was raw and beautiful. This woman was everything he never knew he wanted.

She rubbed against his erection, making him crazy with the need to impale her. Every cell in his body craved to claim her. Somewhere in the back of his mind, a voice tried to remind him she had not agreed.

Carter grabbed the backs of her thighs and carried her to the edge of the patio. He pressed her against the support beam. He slid his hand under her tank top and pulled her breast from its cup. His fingertips pinched her nipple between his finger and thumb, and her head fell back with a moan.

With the kiss broken, he pressed his lips behind her ear, then tasted her skin as he moved down the slim column of her neck. She arched into his palm. Her sexy whimpers filled his dick impossibly full of blood. It pulsed in his pants, begging to go home, wanting to unite them as one.

"Baby." He panted against her ear. "Are you sure you want to do this? If you don't, we need to stop now."

His words came out in a rush, but he was proud he was able to even speak them. His mind was a garbled mess as magic swirled around them. He had never needed to fuck someone so badly in his life, and it would be a fucking of a lifetime. He did not have it in him to make love to her this first time. His nerves were too raw, too needy... too everything.

"Yes, please God, yes! I can't take this anymore. Fuck it all. Just put us out of our misery already." She gasped between raspy breaths, her hips rolling and grinding over him as she searched for the release he would give her.

"There's no turning back," he stated and unwrapped her legs from him. After placing her on shaky legs, he took her face in his hands. "I'm claiming you as mine."

"You belong to me," she stated firmly, her breaths coming hard and fast.

Carter undid her jeans, and she shimmied them down her legs and kicked them aside. He made quick work of doing the same with his. With his pants still wrapped around one ankle, Vanessa jumped into his arms.

"Now, baby. I can't—please, it hurts... Make it better," she cried against his lips.

Blinded by the need to consume her, he ran the tip of his dick across her folds. Finding her primed, he lined them up and let gravity sink her all the way down.

"Shit!" He groaned as a brilliant light flashed around them. The crackle of energy broke his final restraint.

Carter took Vanessa against the column like a madman. She was tight, and warm, and all his. He tucked his face in her neck when she pulled at the hair on his head. Each time he pumped his length into her, he marked her as his one true mate. Nothing ever felt so right, so perfect, or so magical as him fucking her out in the open.

He knew he would not last this first time. Too wound up to stave his impending orgasm, he found her clit between them. Vanessa leaned forward and latched onto his shoulder, her teeth sinking into his flesh but not breaking the skin with the force of her orgasm.

Carter drove into her two more times before he grunted, following her into bliss. His seed spilled deep within her, ruining her for all others as he lay his final claim.

The air around them was thick. Sparks encircled them, and he could almost taste the magic floating around the porch.

"Whoa!" Vanessa said as her outstretched fingers touched a spark. "Are you seeing this?"

He grinned at her childlike awe. "I am." She began to lower her legs, but he stopped her. "Uh-uh. I'm not done with you."

"You're not?" she asked with a mix of surprise and excitement.

Carter shook off his pants and carried her inside. "I've waited too long for this. You're mine until we're both hoarse from screaming."

She ran her fingers through one side of his hair. "I'm pretty sure I didn't scream outside."

He chuckled. "No, and somehow you managed not to draw blood either," he said with a nod toward the teeth mark still marring his skin.

Vanessa's hand flew to her mouth. "Oh my God, I did that?"

Carter climbed onto the bed with Vanessa attached to his front, and he lowered them. Nestled between her silky thighs, he smiled. "You definitely did. Now it's time to take off the rest of your clothes and do all the naughty things we've wanted to do."

He slid her red tank top off over her head and unclasped her bra in a matter of seconds. With her completely bare to him, he did not bother with any niceties and sucked first one nipple and then the next into his mouth.

His cock was ready and eager, even after just coming. Something about this particular woman drove him to new levels. Her fingers found their way back into his hair and massaged his scalp, sending shivers down his body. Every touch she showered him with reached deep within his soul, tangling them further and cementing their connection.

"Fuck me, please," she whimpered.

"Oh, I will, sweetheart," he said around her rosy nipple.

Vanessa moaned and reached between them. Her fingers wrapped around his length and pumped him. His brain short-circuited, and his eyes rolled backward.

"Yes!" he said. "God, your hand feels good."

"My pussy would feel better," she replied.

He paused a moment, not expecting her to talk dirty, but he liked it... *a lot.* Unable to take much more without coming in her hand and not inside her, he pulled back. Looking down at her beautiful face, he kissed the pout from her lips.

Carter kissed everywhere he could before putting them both out of their miseries. Vanessa gasped as she accepted all of him. Carter took his time, savoring the feel of her warm, silky center with long, deep strokes.

He watched her face as she moaned and sighed. Her fingers dug into his ass, urging him to pick up the speed, but he was in no rush. Vanessa was finally his, and nothing would ruin what they were sharing.

Reaching deep within him for control, he changed angles. He hit her G-spot, pressed a thumb to her clit, and rubbed small, tight circles. He wanted to see and feel her come apart. Her pants became shallow, and he knew he had her where he wanted.

"Fuck, yes!" she said.

"Carter." Vanessa groaned as her muscles clamped down around his dick.

His name on her lips as she fell over the edge snapped the little control he held. Lifting her knees high, he gave her everything he had. It wasn't pretty, and it wasn't gentle, but it felt un-fucking-believable.

Their bodies were slick with sweat, and their panting filled the room. He had never experienced anything like it before. Carter had had great sex in his life—no-strings-attached, fun shit—but he knew what they shared could never be described. Amazing was too short of a word for the buildup in his spine.

Looking down at his woman, he watched her face contort with pleasure and her tits bouncing with each thrust. Her hair was stuck to her sweaty face, and she had never looked more beautiful.

Vanessa's lips parted, and her eyes rolled back. The first muscle twitches around his dick warned him of her coming orgasm.

"Look at me, sweetheart," he managed to say between clenched teeth.

The moment their gazes met, the world around them exploded. The sparks outside were nothing compared to the light show their current orgasm had set off in her eyes. When her pupils dilated to a dangerous level, his heart quit beating.

"Vanessa?"

She blinked a few times, her breaths still coming in rapid as they recovered from the mind-blowing orgasm. "Wow," she muttered, her nostrils flaring as she sucked in air.

"Holy shit, I'm tingling everywhere," she said. *"Did I black out? Why's he looking at me like that?"*

He cocked his head and stared. Her lips had not moved, yet he had heard her clear as day. His brows shot up to his hairline.

"Can you hear me?" he asked.

"Of course I can hear you, although my ears are ringing," she said and raised a hand to the side of her head.

"Look at my lips, sweetheart," he demanded. *"You see what our bond did?"*

Her eyes widened. "Whoa! Your lips weren't moving, but I sure as hell heard you!" she said and studied his face.

Carter grinned. "This is crazy."

She nodded and her lids lowered. *"Uh-oh."*

"What's wrong?" he asked.

"For starters, we didn't use a condom. And, you're leaking out of me, so it feels like I'm peeing," she stated, her face scrunching.

He sighed as he removed his length from her. "Hold on, okay?" he said and scooped her into his arms. "We'll get cleaned up, and yeah, I fucked up," he said as he placed her inside his shower. "I'm clean, so you don't have to worry about any venereal diseases. If you want, we can get a morning-after pill," he said and blocked her from the cool water spray. The idea of the pill made his stomach tighten with unease.

"God, she'd be beautiful round with my baby in her," he said.

"What?" she asked, her wide eyes staring at him.

He opened his mouth and shut it once before smiling down at her. Carter caressed her cheek with his thumb. "If you want the pill, we'll get it. You... pregnant with my child? It doesn't scare me, sweetheart. Sure, a pregnancy right now would be a little inconvenient, but it's a blessing I wouldn't turn away."

chapter 27

Her mouth did not seem to work. Her brain had a lot to say on the matter of pregnancy.

I'm not ready. We still need to get to know each other. I'm too young. Holy shit, he's not scared. Oh my God, I'm freaking out.

Then her heart jumped in.

He's ours, and everything will work out like it's supposed to.

The strongest pull and the trump card-holder was her heart. Something told her, her brain would catch up as soon as it was done having a mini stroke.

"You done freaking out yet?" he asked as he pushed to his feet. He had been lathering her body, cleaning her from the mess of their lovemaking as she stood like a pod person.

Vanessa shook her head. "Nope."

He chuckled. "Fair enough," he said before turning her back to the warm spray. His fingers dug in her hair, massaging her scalp as he rinsed the conditioner out. "So, I'm sure it will take some getting used to, but this telepathic thing isn't as bad as I thought."

"Mhmm…" she muttered, losing herself in the relaxing sensation of being pampered by this strong and tender man. Her man.

"I've caught some thoughts while we cleaned up, but I have a strong feeling there's more rattling around in here," he said, his finger tapping the side of her head.

The water pounded at her back when he stepped away to wash himself. Part of her wanted to do it for him, but in that moment, she could not find the energy or focus. The electric spark she always felt in his presence had calmed some, but pregnancy fears aside, she felt different.

"Do you feel… off?" she blurted, her anxiety pressing on her chest.

Carter paused and looked up from his thigh where he was scrubbing. "Off?"

"I must sound crazy," she said.

Glancing down, she noticed he moved faster to finish washing his lower body. When he stood to his full height, her gaze followed his hands as they ran along his length and testicles. She'd just had two life-altering orgasms, and suddenly her sex wept for more of his attention.

"Sweetheart, if you keep looking at my dick like that, I won't be able to answer your question because I'll be balls deep in you."

She sucked in a breath, and her thighs pressed together to alleviate the ache building down below. "Sorry—um…"

He shifted them so he was under the spray, and the suds slid down his body and to the drain. "I don't think you're crazy at all. The telepathic bond is different, and it's strange to hear you but not see your lips move. I'm sure we'll get used to it in time."

She bit her lip, wishing the right words would come to her. Carter shut off the water and wrapped her in a fluffy towel before drying himself. Once the droplets were off both their bodies, he linked their fingers and pulled her back into the bed.

The silence was comfortable, and when he drew her into his side, holding her close to him, he finally spoke. "Outside, the sparks we saw in the air were neat when we became bonded by magic. In here though, it was…"

"Different," she whispered.

Carter shifted onto his elbow and covered her legs with one of his own. "The sparks weren't in the air. They were in your eyes and then your pupils dilated a moment later, unlike anything I've ever seen in my medical profession. To be honest, it scared the shit out of me."

"It did?" she asked.

He nodded and lowered his mouth to hers. "It really did. The orgasm in here was insane. I've never come like that, but I have this… feeling? I don't know how to explain it, but something changed in here. Like *you* changed."

"Me?" she whispered, still unable to sound like the intelligent woman she prided herself to be.

"Yes, sweetheart. Do you feel different?"

"Am I supposed to?"

He shrugged. "Honestly, I don't know. I've never butted into my family's sex life," he said, his lips quirking.

She closed her eyes, thinking back to the moment when her orgasm had consumed her. "Okay, this is probably going to sound strange as hell... You know that moment when you know you're going to come?"

"Yeah?"

She exhaled. "I felt that, but right after, it was like my mind, body, and soul were torn wide open. Just as soon as I felt that, it went away. Ever since, it's like this hum running through me. I feel like my normal self, but different."

He scoffed. "That doesn't sound strange to me at all because about around then was when I saw the bursts of lights in your eyes. And oddly enough, you feel different to me. We'll have to ask my family about it. I'm sure they'll know."

She turned on her side, facing his chest. He smelled of the bodywash and a distinct scent that was all him. His arm came around her and held her tightly, her softness against his hard body. She did not feel self-conscious to lay naked in his arms. She was where she belonged.

"Sleep, baby. We have time for a nap before we need to get ready and leave," he whispered into her damp hair.

His breathing, scent, and warmth lulled her to sleep. Her dreams were filled with varying scenes of water: the beach, waterfalls, rivers, and lakes. The soothing sound of water cascading and washing ashore soothed her senses. Peace settled in her heart and mind until Carter's sweet voice pulled her to the surface.

"Wake up, sleepyhead…"

She turned onto her back and blinked a few times as her eyes adjusted to the afternoon light spilling in. "Mmm… You woke me from a great dream."

Carter plucked her nipple, causing a hiss of pleasure to slip free. "What were you doing in the dream? And was I part of it?"

She giggled. "You were not," she said, enjoying the way his face scrunched and his lips turned down. "I was by myself, surrounded by different kinds of water, and it was peaceful."

He swatted her exposed rear, earning a yelp from her. "That's for making me think you were dreaming with another. Now, up you go. We need to go."

She rubbed the sting from her skin and took his help off the bed. Carter was already wearing his discarded jeans from earlier. His chest and abs were still exposed to her view before he walked into his closet.

"I brought your clothes up. They're in the bathroom," he called.

Vanessa made quick work of getting ready and stared at the mess that was her hair. The one downside to her short hair was it required actual attention. She rushed out to the bathroom she used and set out to blow-drying it. She needed it to look like anything that didn't say: "I just had the best sex of my life and went to bed with wet hair."

Cars lined the driveway and street near Junior's house, clearly indicating they were the last to arrive. It would be the second family dinner she had attended but the first since they had claimed each other.

"Think they'll know?" she whispered as they walked up to the door.

He chuckled. "I'm sure Ethan knew the moment it happened."

She groaned and covered her face with embarrassment.

"Because they know doesn't mean they will say anything."

When they reached the door, Carter let them in to the boisterous sounds of his family chattering. A baby giggled, and the sound of a young girl screaming in delight reached them before they walked into the open room.

"Ay! Look who decided to come after all!" Junior called.

Vanessa pinched his waist. "I thought you said—"

Carter chuckled and whispered in her ear. "He's not. Now quit worrying."

His firm kiss to her temple soothed some of her nerves, until her gaze landed on Ryan. The man's face contorted before he searched the room for his wife. When Brandy took them in, her head cocked to the side as she stopped midsentence in her conversation with Serena.

It continued like that with nearly everyone in the room pausing to stare. The other humans looked on with question, and the children were oblivious to the change in the air.

"What?" Vanessa snapped, unable to take their scrutiny any longer.

"What the hell, guys?" Carter asked as he pulled her tightly against her side.

"Ethan?" Brandy called across the room.

Ethan stepped toward them, his gaze darting back and forth between them until he stood before her. One hand came up in front of him, his palm toward Vanessa, and she forced herself not to withdraw.

"Anyone going to tell me what the hell is going on?" Carter said, his grip tightening around her waist.

"I don't understand it," Ethan muttered and looked up at Carter. "You don't notice it either, do you?"

Brandy appeared at Ethan's side. "I'm sorry, we're not trying to upset either of you. It's just that... You're different," she told Vanessa. "May we?"

"Different how?" she asked before placing a hand in each of their palms.

"I thought you said they wouldn't say anything about how we had sex!" she yelled.

Carter groaned at her side and clasped his head. "That was loud as hell," he muttered, his brows pinching.

"Oh!" Serena said, joining them. "You two... I see."

Vanessa glared up at Carter.

"I don't understand how that happened," Ethan muttered to Brandy.

She shook her head. "Me either."

"For the love of all that's holy, will someone please tell me what the—" Vanessa paused when Katia's big eyes rounded. "What the heck's going on?"

Brandy squeezed her hand and smiled. "Somehow, we all sense magic from *you*."

"And not because you claimed each other," Ethan said, shaking his head.

"Could her magic have been bound? Like yours, Brandy?" Claudia called.

Vanessa shook her head. "That I'm aware of, my parents are run-of-the-mill, boring, middle-class people."

"Do you feel different?" Serena asked.

Vanessa met Carter's eyes, and the worry that had been gnawing on her for the last couple of hours eased.

"Actually, yes. We were hoping to compare notes with weird stuff during... you know."

Ethan squeezed her hand. "Brandy, Serena, or Claudia can help you out there."

The three of them moved to the couch, Carter not far behind as she was sure he wanted to know as well. Brandy turned toward her as Serena kneeled at her feet.

"Well, for us, the only strange thing would have been at the end. When we came, there were sparks of light and our magic pulsed around us. It was beautiful and crazy," Brandy said.

"For us, the magic definitely danced, and there were some sparks. Honestly, I barely remember that part because the next part was rather memorable." Serena smirked and her brows raised suggestively.

"Has anything weird happened since?" Brandy asked. "For me, fire kicked in pretty quick, and I'm an emotional person, so things were going haywire."

Vanessa thought about it for half a second. "No, nothing."

The women nodded and looked up at Carter. "Pay attention and see if anything's changed." Brandy shrugged. "We really can't do anything until we know what we're dealing with."

"I'm *hungwee!*" Katia whined, drawing their attention to the little girl.

"Hey! That is not how we ask for food, young lady," Claudia snapped in her stern mom voice.

Serena chuckled. "Just think what you get to look forward to," she said as she patted Brandy on the back. "Let's eat before Katia has to go scavenging."

The adults in the room chuckled, while the young girl glared with her arms crossed over her chest.

"Whiny or not, having one of them wouldn't be a bad thing at all," Carter said as he helped her from the couch.

chapter 28

Carter leaned on his elbow, enjoying the sway of Vanessa's hips as she moved toward the door. "You know, it would be easier to get dressed if your things were in here," he called.

Her steps faltered, but she never looked back. Once Vanessa was out of line of sight, he dropped to his back and sighed. He did not want to roll out of bed and get ready. No, he wanted to haul his gorgeous woman back into bed and keep her there until she cried out in pleasure at least another three times.

They had made love every night before bed and every morning when they woke. He figured one day, hopefully in the very far future, the need for each other would wane, but until it did, he would lose himself in her as often as he could.

She'd insisted on condoms after the first day they'd had sex. If she was not ready, he had no intention of pushing her. He would only admit to himself that a part of him hoped he had gotten her pregnant the first time. The other part reminded him to not be a caveman about needing to show others his seed was imbedded within her womb.

Baby or not, Vanessa Rayne was his.

Carter rolled out of bed and pushed aside his runaway thoughts. He had not even told her how deep his emotions for her went. He could not bring up a baby and moving in together.

With a quick glance at the time, he made quick work of showering and dressing. With his attention on the button that was making his life a living hell, he heard her approach. He flicked his gaze at the mirror and saw she was leaning against the doorframe in a sexy sundress as she put on a pair of earrings.

"Down, boy, we don't have time for any funny business." She grinned.

"Your mouth is saying one thing, but your eyes are begging me to toss you back into bed," he said, still fighting with the damn button.

Vanessa stepped forward. "Here, let me help you," she said, brushing his fingers away. "I was thinking that maybe today we can swing by the café? I could really eat one of those croissant sandwich thingies. There, all done. No men were harmed in the buttoning of this shirt."

Carter cupped her face and lightly brushed his lips against her red-stained ones. "If that's what you want, then that's what you get, sweetheart."

The smile she graced him with melted his heart. There wasn't anything he would not do for this woman.

It was a crazy thought, considering a few months ago she was not on his radar.

His gaze slid to the rumpled bed, and she chuckled. "Down, boy."

Carter pouted. "I'm sure I'd make it worth your while."

She rolled to her toes and kissed him. "You always do. Now it's time to feed me."

He watched her walk away. "I can't help but think of all the ways I could take you without removing that dress. You're killing me..."

She reached the door to his room and rolled her eyes at him over her shoulder. Carter shook his head and peered down at the obvious tent in his slacks. "Sorry, buddy, she doesn't want to play now."

Laughter down the hall made him smile as he adjusted himself. Vanessa Rayne was the most perfect woman for him. If only the person who wanted her would show their cards, then they could get rid of the danger and fumble through the rest of their get-to-know-you stage without possible death looming over them.

"Who watches baby Gia when Brandy's at work?" Vanessa asked, her eyes on the passing scenery.

He ran his hand up her soft thigh as he glanced from the road to Vanessa and back. "She has a nanny."

"I wonder if it's hard..." she muttered, her words trailing off.

He could almost hear her mind whirling, but whatever she was thinking was not transmitted to him telepathically. "Wonder if what is hard?" he asked.

"Being a working mom."

The corner of his mouth raised. "Ah, that's what this is about. In a couple of weeks, we'll draw some blood if your period doesn't come. But as for your question? I'm not sure. I don't hear Brandy complain, if it helps. I'm sure she'd tell you her pros and cons if you asked."

Her head barely moved in a nod as she disappeared into her thoughts. Carter did not want her to worry, but he left her to it. Everyone deserved to have a moment or two, and he would give her what she needed.

They parked down the street and walked hand in hand to the café. It was still early enough that the morning crowd had not yet come barreling in, demanding their cup of joe. He held open the door for Vanessa and guided her with a hand on her lower back to the register.

One quick look told him Brandy was either not there or back in the office. They placed their order, but before they could walk down to the pickup area, he wrapped a hand above her elbow. "I'm going to the back for a second to see if Brandy's here. Will you be okay?"

She smiled. "I'll be fine."

Grabbing her by the back of her head, he brought their mouths together for a sweet kiss. It was not enough to satisfy him, but what he wanted was not suitable for public consumption. His mouth opened, and when he realized he had nearly professed his love in the middle of the café, he swallowed past the lump in his throat.

"What?" she asked, worry lines forming between her eyes.

He smiled to reassure her. "Have I told you how lucky I am to have you?"

Vanessa's eyes became bright as a grin lit her face. "You have not."

Carter kissed her again. "Well, I am."

As he forced himself to leave her in the middle of the café, two separate individuals joined her among the open seating. With another quick glance over his shoulder, he hurried to the back.

Carter raised a fist and knocked on the door labeled Employees Only. He heard some rustling before Brandy appeared. She looked tired, with bags under her eyes and her hair pulled to the top of her head in some form of bun.

"Car? Everything okay?" she asked and peered around him. "Where's Vanessa? Is she okay?"

He placed a hand on her shoulder. "Whoa, everyone's okay. Are *you* okay?"

Brandy stepped back and waved him in. "Yeah, I'm just exhausted. Gia wasn't having it last night, so I didn't get much sleep."

Carter nodded slowly. "Gotcha, newborn problems. Want me to take a look at her?"

Brandy waved him off. "Nah, she's better now. By the time I realized the kid just needed to fart and couldn't, I was well into zombie mode."

He chuckled. "You should get some gas drops. A lot of parents find they help."

She tilted her head. "Thanks, I'll have Ryan pick them up. I don't need a part two to last night. Now, what do I owe the pleasure of—"

A loud bang sounded outside the office, and his heart plummeted as Brandy's eyes widened. "Vanessa!"

They stormed out of the office as people cried out in surprise. Carter turned the corner, and a woman's scream pierced the air. He called himself a hundred different names for leaving Vanessa alone and vulnerable. Sure, she seemed to be exuding magic, but any magic she could do was new and unrefined. She was sure to cause more harm than good if she tapped into it without learning to control it.

Tables and chairs lay skewed in various directions of the floor. Vanessa stood in the middle as a woman crouched against the counter behind her. The few early employees could not be seen, as steam gushed from one machine.

Carter's quick scan of the room returned to Vanessa and a half human, half dog before her. If Carter had never borne witness to a werewolf, he would have mistakenly believed that thing was one. He stepped forward, intending on protecting her, when a small hand gripped his bicep.

"No! I've got her," Brandy hissed before she rushed forward.

He felt her surge of power before she took three steps and grimaced. The spells he now wielded for telekinesis were no match for the thing threatening Vanessa. As much as he wanted to step in, he swallowed his pride and let Brandy do what he could not.

His magic swirled around him, begging to protect his mate, when he remembered their tethered minds.

"Vanessa... Sweetheart, are you okay?" he asked.

When no reply came, he scanned the room again. He could no longer hear the steam from the machines or the cries from the humans. In fact, it seemed the air itself was stagnant.

"Brandy?" he called as she placed a hand on Vanessa.

"It's okay. Go to Carter, and he'll heal you," she said as Vanessa's shoulders sagged, and a gasp pierced the silent room.

Vanessa turned on her heels, her eyes darting around before they locked on his. The blood in his veins boiled at the red line running from her shoulder and down her collar bone to her breastbone. The gash was not deep, but blood seemed to pour from it.

"Fuck," he snapped when she reached his arms and crumbled.

"Carter," she said through a heavy breath, and her eyes flickered. Her long, dark lashes fanned as her lids tried to close yet remain open.

He shifted her in his arms and lowered them to the ground. Vanessa had his entire focus when he placed one hand on her wound, ignoring his years of training that told him to avoid her blood. Carter released his magic and tried to ignore the similarities to Tyler's wounds months ago. His brows pinched as he drained himself into her.

"Brandy!" he cried when Vanessa barely healed.

Noises boomed around them as Brandy called back, "Car?"

"What the hell is going on?" a woman asked, her phone in hand as she recorded the mess.

Carter met Brandy's eyes as she raised one hand in the air.

"No, wait! I think I can help," a woman called.

Everything became muted once more as Brandy froze the café and hurried toward him, with the woman in tow. "What's wrong?" Brandy asked, her eyes flitting nervously toward the woman.

At that moment, he did not care if every human in the city witnessed him heal, so long as he could make Vanessa better again. "It's not working," he stated, emotions clogging his throat.

"Did the lycan do that?" the woman asked, cementing she knew about their supernatural world.

Carter nodded.

The woman pinched her lips and looked around. She spotted something in the open cooler, and he watched her run to it and return with a bottle of spring water. She twisted the cap and tipped the bottle over Vanessa's growing wound.

"Here, now get her to drink some," the woman ordered.

"I'm not sure that's going to—" Brandy gasped as he poured the water into Vanessa's mouth. "What the hell is in that water?"

He had heard his sister clearly, but he was too focused on Vanessa to ask any sort of clarifying questions. Indeed, the wound on her chest began to heal, and within seconds, her lids fluttered again.

With her recovery, all his other senses came online.

chapter 29

"She needs to drink more," a woman ordered, and a bottle pressed against Vanessa's lips.

She did not know what was happening. Was she in hell? Heaven? Some other alternate reality for witches' mates?

One minute, she was looking at her phone and waiting on her croissant sandwich while Carter went to look for Brandy, and the next, she was being ripped open. The painful memory had her touching the skin, now raised and wet, as she swallowed another mouthful of water.

She pushed the bottle away and sat up. Brandy, Carter, and the woman stared back. It was the woman Vanessa had noticed when she and Carter had first entered because of the flower in her wavy hair.

"Are you okay?" Brandy asked.

"Sweetheart, how do you feel?" Carter asked.

The woman offered Vanessa a kind smile as she replied to the others. "What happened?"

"You didn't sense him when he came in. I didn't think he'd attack with all the humans here, but he didn't seem to care."

"Who are you?" Brandy asked.

"I'm Mia," she said, absently glancing at the still room. "We should probably do something about *him* before you risk shorting your magic."

Mia's beauty was ethereal and made Vanessa think of mystical beings like sprites, pixies, and nymphs. Energy pulsed from her the same as it did from Carter and Brandy, something Vanessa was beginning to notice and assign to witches. She was not sure when she started feeling the distinction, but there, on the floor of Brandy's café, half lying on Carter with Brandy and Mia kneeling at her side, she knew the difference.

Mia offered Brandy a hand after rising to her feet. The woman smirked when Brandy ignored her hand and rose.

"No offense," Brandy muttered and brushed past Mia.

Through Carter, Vanessa had learned that his sister was one of the most powerful witches around—if not *the* most powerful. Mia probably sensed it, but she did not show any signs of being bothered in the slightest over the fact.

The lycan's face unfroze, his bloody claw still outstretched. "What the—"

"No more fucking games. You just came into a café filled with humans and attacked her," Brandy snapped, one hand pointing at Vanessa as her face remained focused on the lycan. "Why? And don't you give me some sort of bullshit answer, because contrary to popular belief, I can do this all fucking day," she said.

Mia chuckled at Brandy's side. "Just give the lady what she wants, or else…"

Something swirled in Mia's palm, and Vanessa could not tell what it was from where she sat, but it looked like some sort of plant. Whatever it was, the lycan's growl reverberated through the café as his head tipped back.

"Olsabir. Word got back to him about some human running her mouth," he replied.

The women shared a look before Mia peered back at Vanessa. "I think his nose is broken. She's no human."

His nostrils flared, and his eyes glowed. "That doesn't make any sense. It's the same woman."

"Guess you should have sniffed before attacking," Brandy said. "Now, I have to remove *you* from the picture for exposing us all to these humans."

He attempted to struggle, but with the magical hold on him, it was futile. Vanessa did not see Brandy twitch—let alone move—and the lycan went up in flames. There one minute, gone the next.

She flicked a finger, and a gust of wind carried the ashes out the front door. Carter helped Vanessa to her feet as Brandy righted all the tables and chairs before placing her hands on her hips. "Shit, what do we do about them?"

"I can help with that," Mia said with a wink.

They watched her produce a small vial as she moved toward the closest human. She tipped the liquid onto a finger and rubbed whatever it was on their temple. Mia moved around the room and repeated the action as they watched on with curiosity.

"There, they won't remember the last twenty minutes with how much I gave them. It may cause some problems with orders, but their memories will be lycan-free," Mia said, joining the three of them.

Brandy nodded slowly and Vanessa could only stare, a thousand questions bouncing around her head. The wound on her chest was merely a memory, and Carter's firm hold anchoring her to him was a reminder of the fear they had all felt.

"Let's take care of whatever this phone might have captured," Brandy said, hurrying to the woman with her phone in hand.

It was not lost on Vanessa that Carter's healing powers had not worked on her for some reason. Glancing away from the women and to his handsome face, she could still see his fear in his expression.

The sounds in the café returned, and people cleared their throats. They all shared a look, embarrassment and confusion clouding their faces before their gazes snapped down to their hands.

"It worked," Brandy whispered, her curious eyes taking in Mia. "Who are you?"

Mia offered a hand. "Mia Hemlock."

They each took a turn shaking her hand, and Carter and Brandy continued their scrutiny of the woman. Vanessa did not know what they were looking for or what Vanessa was missing, but it was clear that whatever Mia had done was new to them.

Carter cleared his throat. "Thank you... I don't understand why I couldn't—"

Mia's smile was soft when she faced Vanessa. "She's not like us."

A week ago, she was a human, then she was not. What the hell was she?

"I don't understand, if I'm not human—"

Brandy cleared her throat and smiled at a man whose pinched brows were directed at them. "No one feels human in the morning." She chuckled and waved them toward the back.

"Sorry," Vanessa whispered and followed Brandy into a small room in the back she had never noticed. "I'm not human? And I'm not like you guys?" she asked, giving Mia a sideways glance. "Am I on some wanted list then? Did they take a candid of me, because how the hell do they even know who to look for?" she snapped, her strength returning.

Carter squeezed her hand in support. "How did you know about the water? What aren't you telling us?"

"Yes, while I'm grateful for your help, please cut to the chase," Brandy replied.

"Why don't you just tell them?" Mia asked Vanessa. "I mean, I get why the secrecy and all—"

"Oh my God, because *I* don't know. Until a week or so ago, no one thought I was anything more than a curious human."

Mia's brows narrowed as she shook her head. "That doesn't make sense."

Vanessa tossed her hands in the air. The woman was the first person to have any clue about what was going on with Vanessa, and she was not giving her any information. "No shit. Now, please," she said with a wave of her hand to move along.

"You're a nymph, a naiad based on how quickly you healed from the water."

"A what?" Vanessa asked before Mia even finished.

"Aren't they just Greek mythology?" Brandy asked.

Mia nodded. "I don't think there are many alive. Those that are live in hiding," she told Brandy before her attention shifted to Vanessa. "Nymphs are spirits of nature and really rare to find."

"So how are you so sure I'm one?" Vanessa asked.

A shadow crossed her face. "I used to know one, so I know how to identify their unique magic. I'm guessing you two sensed it but couldn't seem to put your finger on what it was."

"Why couldn't I heal her? I've been able to heal lycan bites before. I don't understand," Carter said.

Mia shrugged. "Nymphs don't follow the same magical rules. They can, however, heal themselves if they have access to earth or water. That's why I poured it directly on her wound and had you help her drink."

"What was in the vial?" Brandy asked, and Vanessa stopped herself from pouting at the change in topic. She wanted to know more about nymphs, but it appeared she would have to wait a little longer.

"Oil from the peyote plant. Its hallucinogenic properties make it easier to use a mind-erasing spell. Gentle and effective on the human mind," she said.

Carter stiffened at her side. "You gave those people oil from a hallucinogenic plant?"

Mia's eyes rounded. "I did. Feel free to go check on them and see every single person is okay. Once you get down from your high horse, you can ask me nicely for some. I'm assuming you're in the healthcare field, and one day you're going to expose yourself by using your supernatural healing," she stated, a brow raised to her hairline.

The woman was kind but had a hard edge to her. Vanessa could very easily become her friend. Carter released her hand and slipped out to check on the customers, leaving the three women alone.

Brandy chuckled when the door shut. "I should be upset at how you spoke to my brother, but I'm not. What else can you tell us about Vanessa?"

Mia bit her lower lip as she shook her head. "Not much more to say. Your nymph magic isn't super strong, so if you didn't know, my guess is that you're only half nymph. When did you guys notice a change in her? Something must have drawn out her magical side."

Vanessa felt her cheeks warm.

"She's my brother's mate, and they bonded," Brandy replied hurriedly, saving Vanessa from telling the stranger herself.

Mia nodded, her face scrunching in deep thought. "And she wasn't exhibiting any magic beforehand?"

Vanessa should be annoyed they were speaking as if she was not there in the room with them, but she couldn't bring up the emotion. Her nerves and mind were glitching out with each morsel of information. If she was half nymph, then it meant one of her parents was a nymph. The fact that neither had ever brought up the possibility she would eventually tap into her magic said one of two things. Either they were assholes who kept things from her, or there was a chance that whoever knew had never shared it with the other.

"No, the closest thing would have been the soul mate link between her and Carter," Brandy said, and he returned on cue.

"Everything okay with the patients?" Mia teased.

Carter pulled Vanessa to his side, and she wrapped an arm around his waist. She wanted his strength as everything she had thought about her world became one heaping pile of lies.

"They're fine, although I'm surprised they're not exhibiting any strange effects from the drug," he said.

Mia scoffed. "That's because it's not a drug. It's an herb. I also didn't give them a lot. I was trying to help erase their memory, not pulverize their brains."

"Mia thinks Vanessa is half nymph. It would explain why no one noticed, not that I would have since I thought they only existed in folklore," Brandy told Carter.

Carter peered down. "You had no idea?"

Vanessa shook her head. "Not one clue. My parents have a lot of explaining to do."

chapter 30

Vanessa was a nymph.

Carter did not know what it meant exactly or what it would entail. As long as she was safe and remained his, he really didn't care.

Mia still left him uneasy, mostly because he did not know her. Carter didn't trust easily, and it seemed something new was often being thrown his way as of late. His family alone had nearly doubled in size in the last year.

"Carter?" Vanessa called. From her tone, he realized it was not for the first time.

"Hmm?"

She rose to an elbow and looked down at him. Her hair stuck up this way and that in a sexy post-sex mess. "I asked if this changed anything?"

With her post-orgasm haze no longer evident in her eyes, he sensed her worry. "If being part nymph changed anything between us, you mean?"

Her nod was barely perceptible as she chewed on the inside of her cheek.

Carter cupped her face and smiled. "It doesn't change a damn thing. You belong to me, and I belong to you, sweetheart. You could sprout horns and I'd still love you—"

His words slipped free on their own accord, leaving him skating on uneven ground. Her eyes widened, and her next words surprised him.

"I'm going to sprout horns?"

All nerves from his confession vanished at the incredulous look on her face, and he burst into laughter. Vanessa smacked him in the shoulder, hard, her angry eyes staring at him.

"Don't laugh at me! I know barely anything about nymphs, and—"

He pushed up and kissed the words from her mouth. "Did you not hear everything I said?"

"Yes, you said I could sprout horns and you'd still lo—" Her mouth formed a cute little O. "You love me?"

He chuckled at her incredulous tone. "I do, very much."

Carter barely got the words out before she climbed atop him and took his mouth in a searing kiss. He moved his hands from her hips up her sides as his dick stirred to life. It was impossible not to react to her sex, warm and wet, pressed against his cock.

Vanessa broke their kiss and peered down to where their bodies met. "Again?"

Carter thrust his hips. "You're the one who climbed on top, sweetheart."

Her giggle wrapped around his heart and squeezed. The woman turned him into a lovesick puppy. He would never admit it to anyone, but behind closed doors, when it was just the two of them, he knew it was the truth.

Only Carter and Vanessa mattered—not their families, magic, or whatever supernatural being was creating plans to find her. It was just the two of them. If he could live within the bubble they created when they crawled into bed, he would.

"What did you expect when you told me you love me?" she asked.

He chuckled when she rolled her eyes. "Your undying love to be honest, but I'll take whatever you're offering," he said, running his now-hard length through her folds.

Vanessa moaned as she arched. Her head lolled back, and her breasts pushed toward him. "I think I've loved you since the moment we touched."

Her words washed over him in a caress. He was barely able to focus yet eager to make love to her now that the whole truth had been laid bare. Carter made quick work of the second condom within reach. Fully sheathed, he lifted her hips and brought her down onto him.

It was quick but raw. They professed their love with their bodies as they each spoke the words over and over again. He thought sex with Vanessa had been intense before, but he was wrong.

Their orgasms ripped through them. Gasping for breath and slick with sweat, he struggled to form a single thought past the need to make her his in every way. Carter bit his tongue, afraid to ruin the moment with a rushed proposal. He did not think Vanessa would be as quick as him to agree to a handfasting.

He set the thought aside. Now knowing it was his end goal, he had plenty of time to perfect whatever plans he could concoct.

"Wow." Vanessa panted and became limp in his arms. "I didn't think that could get any better."

Carter kissed her head and pat the hair down from tickling his face. "Everything with you is better."

A little giggle rumbled against his chest from hers before her breaths became even. He wondered if she even cared their bodies were still connected. Carter had no intention of rushing them apart. He was exactly where he belonged.

***

"Are you sure you want me there?" Carter asked for the third time. He pointed toward the car with his thumb. "I can come back and pick you up or even stay in the car."

Vanessa looked from the house to him and shook her head. "Please?" she whispered, and he hated the tremble he heard.

He pulled her against his chest and held her tight. "Okay, sweetheart."

Carter did not want to meet her parents under these circumstances, not even a little bit. But there was no way he would leave her to do it alone if she wanted him there.

Pulling back, he cupped her face. "You can do this." He lowered his mouth to hers and imagined his strength and pride seep into the kiss.

When their eyes met, he noted the fear in hers had lessened. "Here goes everything," she told him and linked their fingers together. "They might not even be home."

Her wobbly smile made him chuckle. "Liar," he said

He squeezed her hand after knocking on the door. When she shifted from foot to foot at his side, he pressed his lips to her temple. "Breathe—"

Locks disengaged and the doorknob turned. "Vanessa?"

She was an older version of Vanessa but with shoulder-length hair. Her smile faltered, and her brows pinched as she studied Vanessa.

"Hi, Mom. Carter, I'd like you to meet my mom, Daphyne. Mom, Carter's my—" Vanessa paused and worried her lip.

Carter released her hand and offered it. "Her boyfriend," he said without skipping a beat.

Vanessa's eyes softened as her mother's hardened.

"Pleasure meeting you," he said, infusing all the charm he could muster in the words.

"Boyfriend?"

"Yes." Vanessa cocked her head. "Can we come in, or are you going to keep us outside?"

Her mother eyed him again before forcing a smile as she stepped aside. Vanessa released his hand and hugged her mother. The woman's eyes, a mossy green, flashed at the contact, and an apologetic expression grazed her features before she regained her composure.

"I can make some tea, as it seems we have a lot to talk about," Daphyne said, giving Carter a knowing look.

"Where's Dad?" Vanessa asked ahead of them.

"He's bowling, honey. His league is practicing for their next game."

They moved down a hall, passed a formal living room and bedrooms off another hall, and stopped at a small dining room off the kitchen. The home was decorated in whites and beige colors. Various plants were the only thing to bring color and life to the rooms.

Taking Vanessa's lead, he stood beside her as she leaned forward on the edge of a kitchen counter. He was tempted to run a hand over her back but did not want to upset her mother any more than she was.

Daphyne worked on the tea, keeping her hands busy as she updated Vanessa on her dad's success at bowling. The small talk gave Carter time to observe her and the humble home she kept.

Everything was like the home and mother Vanessa had described to him on the way over—if he did not count the huge secret lying between them. Carter attempted to push out his magic, curious to see if he noticed anything.

Before he could reach Daphyne, he was slammed against a wall with vines wrapped around each wrist and ankle. The force of his back hitting the wall pushed air from his lungs, and he knew his eyes gave away his surprise.

Vanessa screamed as she rushed to his side.

"Get away from him, Vanessa," Daphyne demanded.

Vanessa pushed to her feet and slammed her hands on her hips. "No. If you're doing this, stop it right now!"

"He's dangerous," she countered, her eyes flashing green.

Vanessa caressed his face. "Well, that answers our question."

Carter chuckled and pressed a kiss to her palm. It took everything in him to remain calm. He was chained to a damn wall by vines, not something he had anticipated by visiting Vanessa's parents.

"Told you I should have stayed in the car," he joked.

"I didn't know she was going to lose her shit," she said and shook her head. *"I mean, it's clear she's the nymph."*

"I kind of wish I had this trick. I'd have fun having my way with you," he teased.

Vanessa flushed at his words, but the smile at her lips spoke volumes.

"What are—oh my God, you two are soul mates?"

The hold on his body released as quickly as it had come. Carter rubbed his wrists and pushed a little magic into his wounds. Vanessa ran her hands down him, searching for any signs of injury.

"I'm okay, sweetheart."

Relief pushed the worry from her gaze before her hand waved between him and her mom. "What the hell was that? Why would you do that? I mean, it's clear you've been hiding your nymph side from me, but attacking Carter for no reason? Does Dad know? Is he also a nymph? Better start explaining, Mom, because I'm done with all the secrets and lies!"

Carter was both impressed and amused by her little speech. The fire in her reminded him of Brandy whenever he or his brothers interfered in her life. They did so out of pure love, of course, but she never cared about the why.

"I..." Daphyne looked between them, and her shoulders sagged. "I'm sorry, honey."

"Sweetheart, maybe you can tell her how we met and everything else to give her time to find the right words."

"Are you defending her?"

Surprise filled him when she turned on him. Carter cleared his throat to stop from becoming amused. "Pretty sure all I suggested was that you start first."

Vanessa sighed. "Oh, right."

He wrapped an arm around her shoulders and guided her to a couch thirty feet away. Carter suspected it would be a long chat, and they needed whatever they could get to calm the mood.

Daphyne followed at a safe distance, with their tea on a tray. Once they settled, Vanessa started. He listened to the familiar story and watched Daphyne's reactions.

Sadness, surprise, anger, and a few emotions he could not pinpoint flitted across her face. Her eyes rolled, and she shifted uncomfortably when Vanessa glossed over them sealing their mate status.

"Something in me changed but no one could figure it out, at least not until a lycan attacked me and Carter was unable to heal me. Thankfully, Mia recognized what I was and saved me..."

chapter 31

Vanessa's anxiety rose with each passing second of silence.

Her mom cleared her throat. "I didn't know..."

Vanessa pressed closer to Carter, drawing in his heat and comfort. "Know what?"

"That you were like me. I kept a close eye on you, but when it was clear you took after your father, I quit worrying. If I'd known, I would have prepared you."

"Is Dad—"

She shook her head. "No, honey. He's not. I met him long ago and broke all the rules when I fell in love with a human. When I chose him, I knew I couldn't tell him or I'd risk putting him in danger." Daphyne sighed. "I'm so sorry. I know not telling you put you in danger, but if your magic hadn't kicked in, telling you would have been just as dangerous. When you and Georgia became best friends, I knew she'd be forced to keep her secret, but I knew you were safe."

Carter scoffed behind her. "You pinned me to the wall for being a witch but think a werewolf is safer?"

"I pinned you to the wall because you were using your magic in my home. Georgia is a part of the Alumbra pack, and they've always behaved themselves in the highest regards. There was no question Vanessa would be safe near them, as a human or nymph. I should say half nymph."

Vanessa turned in his arms. "You used your magic?"

Carter nodded. "I did. I wanted to see if I sensed anything. It's not like I was going to go defensive."

"We both know I can't," he told Vanessa.

"I don't understand," her mom said.

"Tell her," she pleaded.

Carter sighed. "I can only heal and push out my magic to sense. My sister-in-law has been teaching me spells, but until I know them better, I can't do more."

Daphyne shook her head. "Either you're lying or you're wrong."

"Mom!" Vanessa snapped.

"Listen," Daphyne replied. "I don't mean to insult, but I felt your magic the moment you were in front of me. As a full-blooded nymph, my link to earth is powerful, and I knew you were a witch immediately." Daphyne turned to Vanessa. "I expect you will find yourself drawn to all things earth as well, honey."

"What *can* you do, Mom?"

Daphyne pushed to her feet, moved before them, and spun once. As she did, her clothes transformed. Gone was her blouse and khaki capris. Instead, a beautiful gown made of leaves, flowers, and moss covered her. Flowers and leaves decorated her head, casting a beautiful glow around her face. Vines wrapped around her arms and to her fingers, and a veil ran down her back to the ground. Before them stood a stunning ethereal creature, and gone was her mother.

"Follow me," she said in a soothing singsong voice, replacing what Vanessa had always identified as her mother's.

Vanessa pushed to her feet and followed, admiring the beautiful cape running down her mother's back and to the ground. Carter's warm hand rested on her lower back, anchoring her to the present.

She had never seen anything as beautiful as her mother. "Where are we going?"

"You'll see."

They walked onto the patio and neared her mother's modest garden. With each step Vanessa took, she could feel the magic in the air thicken. Her hand flew toward her face and swatted at a spiderweb she hadn't noticed, praying the spider was not crawling about her head.

Carter gasped at her side, and she opened her eyes to see what had made him react. "Where are we?"

Daphyne grinned. "My secret garden, of course."

Vanessa spotted a waterfall in the distance and could hear a brook bubbling nearby. Trees as tall as the sky covered them from the sun. Various bushes, plants, and flowers surrounded them in paradise.

"It's beautiful," Vanessa whispered, afraid to disturb the peace engulfing them. "Are we still in the yard?"

"Yes and no. The spiderweb you felt wasn't real. You stepped through the portal I opened. This was my first home and where I met your father. He'd been out hiking when I first saw him." A smile lit her face at the memory. "I was drawn to him, and before I knew it, I'd taken on the form of a human."

She spun in a circle, her arms stretched wide. "This is your legacy, honey—one I'd given up hope that you'd ever receive. I can teach you how to hone your magic and how to open a portal here. You must believe me when I say I never wanted to keep this from you."

Vanessa rushed forward and wrapped her arms around her mom. Hundreds of butterflies suddenly flew around them, causing Vanessa to step back. "Whoa, where'd they come from?" She giggled.

Carter chuckled. "They were her cape."

"Nature is as a part of me as the oxygen we breathe. Follow me," Daphyne told them and padded to the pool of water at the base of the waterfall. "Witches haven't always been good to my kind. When I sensed you were a witch, I felt your love for Vanessa but didn't know if you were being deceptive. I apologize for expecting the worst from you." She pointed at the water. "I want you both to drink. It is my gift to you and your union."

Carter and Vanessa shared a glance, unsure about the crystal-clear water.

"You are mates, honey. I wouldn't dare interfere with the goddess's plan."

Carter knelt first, scooped water into his hand, and offered it to her. Vanessa joined him on her knees and sipped. She had never tasted water so pure in her life. Carter did it again and drank the refreshing liquid.

Warmth spread within her, and the colors around them became bright, too bright. Vanessa covered her eyes and fell onto her bottom. "What's happening?"

A voice in the distance spoke, but she could not make out the words. Fear and anxiety filled her. "Carter?" she called, but even to her own ears, his name did not sound right.

Her senses exploded. Each blade of grass prickled her skin, helicopter blades sounded, and a million smells fought for her attention, so she refused to open her eyes to the bright light threatening to burn through her eyelids.

And then everything went black.

***

Hushed voices caught her attention as she breathed in Carter's cologne-and-musk scent. His body was warm and rigid under hers. She sensed his concern and anger. The fabric under her cheek was soft, and his cargo pants felt rough against the backs of her thighs.

Her tongue felt thick. "C-Carter?"

"Shh... It's okay, sweetheart, give it a moment." He ran a hand through the hair at the side of her head.

"What happened?" she asked, parting her lids, so light could begin to assault her eyes.

"How are you feeling?" he asked.

"Alive," she said, noting how loudly her nerves fired within her.

"Just give it a second, honey."

Her mom. Vanessa then remembered where they were. Once she forced her eyes to open all the way, she narrowed them on her mother. She'd returned her appearance to what Vanessa had remembered her to be. She wore her blouse, khaki capris, and her hair in place. "What did you do?"

"I—"

Carter squeezed her tightly against his chest. "How do you feel, sweetheart?"

Vanessa pushed against his chest and faced her mother. "What the hell was in that water?"

"The water is healing. In both of your cases, it will draw out any of your hidden magic."

"You could have warned us!" Vanessa tried to stand but found herself back in Carter's lap.

His fingers dug into her hips. "You okay?"

Vanessa sucked in a deep breath. "Still kind of woozy."

"Honey, I didn't know it would affect you like that."

Vanessa looked over her shoulder at Carter. "How did you react?"

He shook his head. "Not like you. It made my skin feel like an electric current ran along it, and it felt like the world was tipped on its axis. Didn't last long."

Vanessa pressed a hand to her head. "Every single one of my senses went nuts. I know it's crazy, but I feel like I'm still by the waterfall."

Her mother grinned. "Not crazy at all. That's actually really great news. It means it worked. You'll be forever connected to that spot. Your senses are on overdrive, but they will calm down. I think you've reacted so strongly because you're not a full-blooded nymph, honey. I'm sorry, I should have anticipated that."

She raised a brow at her mom before deciding to relax against Carter. He was home, and his body and scent wrapped her in a cocoon of love and protection.

"I was telling your mom more about the lycan and what he said," Carter told her before pressing his lips on the spot where her neck and shoulder met.

"Honey, while demons are a threat to witches, werewolves, and other supernatural beings, they aren't to us—at least not to me. Your half breed status I'm not sure of because I don't know a lot about it."

"Why?"

"Simply put, we're more powerful."

chapter 32

Carter could not reconcile the woman before him with the one in the enchanted forest. "How old *are* you?"

Vanessa's elbow connected with his ribs. "Carter!"

He sucked in a breath and shot Daphyne an apologetic smile. "Sorry, it's just—"

Daphyne raised a hand. "It's quite all right. You both should hear this. I don't age. I'm two hundred and thirty-seven years old."

"Wha—I mean, that's not possible, Mom. You have gray hairs, and there are wrinkles along your eyes that weren't there even five years ago!"

Daphyne's eyes twinkled with mischief before they watched her age before their eyes. Gone was the middle-aged woman, and in her place was a woman in nearly her nineties.

"Whoa!" they exclaimed before she returned to her previous age.

"I have to make myself look the part. If I didn't, I'd put your father and myself in danger. It was a decision I made when I fell in love with him."

Vanessa leaned forward. "What's your true form then?"

"The one you saw by the waterfall. Now that you've drunk from the spring, I suspect you, too, won't age. I promise to help you adjust to your powers. Listen though, *no* human can learn of this."

Vanessa bit her lip and shook her head as she peered at Carter. "That's not possible."

Power filled the air, similar to when Brandy would tap into her magic. "Why not? Our lineage is to be protected at all costs. How can you tell me it's not possible?"

Carter could understand how a nymph was potentially stronger than a demon. "I have two sisters-in-law who are human. They know of my family and know she has magic. By now, they're sure to know she's a nymph."

Daphyne jumped to her feet and faced Vanessa. "How could you be so stupid as to let humans know of us!"

Magic flowed through him. Power like he had never felt seeped into each cell at her words. "Watch your words, Daphyne! I won't have you speaking to her in that way. Do you hear me? Vanessa understands how imperative it is to keep our secret."

Carter barely recognized his own voice. His body pulsed in a way similar to when he healed. He was pissed at her for calling his mate stupid. Vanessa was anything but, and no one would speak to her that way so long as he lived.

"Baby?" Vanessa asked, her hand featherlight against his skin.

He turned at the endearment, surprised to hear it. She fixed her steady eyes on him, and a wave of calm hit him. She was his world.

Vanessa pointed around the room. "Look."

He followed her gaze and stared with surprise. Things floated in the air: couches, lamps, books, and trinkets. Pissed or not, he didn't want to damage any of Daphyne's things. He mentally commanded the couches to lower, and one by one, he set the other things down. With her belongings settled, Carter couldn't help but wonder if their trip to the garden had anything to do with his magic going haywire at his outburst.

He faced Daphyne. "The water?"

"Yes."

He inhaled deeply and nodded. "I'd kindly ask that you never speak to Vanessa in that manner. I can promise you, the members of my family, witch or human, would never risk my mate—nymph or not."

"You're right. I apologize—"

"Don't apologize to me, apologize to *her*," he stated firmly and pulled Vanessa's back to his front.

"Honey, I'm sorry. Carter's right, it was unkind and unfair of me to speak so harshly to you. Please understand, I'm not used to this. I haven't discussed my secret with anyone in many, many years."

He sat, and Vanessa cuddled into his side. "Is there anything you can tell us about a demon named Olsabir?" he asked. "He's the one who's sending people after Vanessa."

"Olsabir?" She laughed. "He's a pussy."

"Mom!"

"Show him your true power, and he'll back off. That bastard only cares about keeping humans in the dark so he can swindle them and do other works under their noses. The moment you show him your true power, he'll leave you alone. I'd offer to do it myself, but it has to come from you, Vanessa."

"Do you have any ideas on how I can confront him?" Vanessa asked, her thumb rubbing his stomach.

"First you need to get a handle on your powers. You mentioned your senses being on overdrive. We need to take advantage of it while we can. Soon, everything will calm down, and while you can still learn, I think doing it now will help you faster."

"*I think I should see Serena or Brandy about my own. Will you be okay if I come back to get you?*" he asked.

"Will you have time to help me now? I mean, when is Dad due home?"

Daphyne twisted her wrist and nodded. "He'll be back in an hour. I'll leave him a note saying I went for a walk. It's best to take you back to the spring anyhow."

"Carter, can you pick me up later?" Vanessa asked.

"Oh, I can drop you off at home, honey. It's no problem."

Vanessa cleared her throat. "I—um... I've been staying with Carter. You know, since this whole mess."

Daphyne's brow raised. "I'm sure you have..."

A blush heated Carter's face. With his mother passing when he was very young, he had avoided all embarrassing sex talks. His father had kept things brief, emphasizing sex with the right woman would be magical. He'd strategically left out any mention of their witch lineage.

Carter pushed to his feet and offered Vanessa a hand. "I'll come back. Just let me know when."

She rose to her tiptoes and brushed her lips against his softly. He wanted to deepen it but managed to hold back in front of her mother.

Vanessa caught his eyes with her own and smiled. "I love you."

Carter brushed her hair from her face as he filled with complete joy. "I love you too," he whispered back before addressing them both. "I will see myself out. Have fun, ladies."

He went out the way they had come in and stopped by his car. The house was like all the others on the street, a normal middle-class home, welcome garden flags, and decorative gnomes in the flower beds. Nothing screamed magic or nymph to a passerby.

He unlocked the car, slid into the seat, and headed to Serena's. He was eager to learn what other powers the water had unlocked. Carter made a mental note to leave out the spring and the beautiful forest they'd visited.

He trusted Serena, but the others who worked or shopped there weren't family. Carter would do everything to keep Daphyne's secret contained, as it also protected Vanessa.

Later, the bell chimed as he pushed open the door, and the now-familiar smell of sage filled his lungs.

"Carter?" Brandy called from Serena's side.

Both women took him in with curious stares.

"Hi, ladies," he said and wove his way around tables to the counter where they were gathered.

Serena kissed his cheek, and Brandy asked, "Is Vanessa okay?"

After Carter hugged Brandy, he peered around the shop. "Yeah, she's okay. I didn't expect to find you here, Bran."

"Yeah, I came for a visit before going to pick up Gia. Why'd *you* swing by?"

"Are we alone?" he asked Serena.

The three of them looked around and she nodded. "Need me to close?"

He nodded, and the lock on the door sounded. Carter glanced at the closed sign swaying in the window and grinned.

"Let's go upstairs so you can share what this is all about," Serena commanded, and with a swish of her long skirt, she hurried toward the curtain.

Carter put his arm around his sister's shoulders, and they followed the high priestess side by side, until the narrow stairs forced him to usher her ahead.

As per her usual routine, Serena asked for their tea preference and prepared it as Brandy and he moved to the couch. He took the time to ask about the café, Gia, and Ryan, anything to root him to the normal lives they lived.

The tea kettle whistled, and they returned to the small kitchen. Serena passed each of them a mug as a noise came from the stairs. He looked at the women, who only shrugged. When he turned, he found Ethan with Ryan at his heels.

"Really?" Carter asked, eyeing the two women.

Ethan stepped toward Carter for a brotherly hug. "Don't get on them. Rye was already with me, and you weren't answering your phone."

Carter pulled back. His brows pinched before drawing his cell from his back pocket. Three missed calls and over ten texts flashed on his notifications. "I didn't hear it, sorry."

"Where'd you go?" Ethan demanded. "One second I felt you, and the next you didn't exist and then bam, you were back. It was the strangest thing."

"Let's go sit. This kitchen is too damn small for all of us," Serena called.

Once they settled, Carter told them about meeting Daphyne and hesitantly mentioned the portal she had created to the forest. He revealed Daphyne had given them something to drink, leaving out the spring and how it had messed with his magic.

"Are you okay?" Brandy asked.

Carter stared back at the four sets of eyes watching him carefully. "I *feel* fine, but it seems I won't be needing spellwork to tap into telekinesis anymore. I came here hoping Serena would help me figure out how to access it and to figure out if any other magical abilities were awakened."

Serena chuckled, and the sound was musical. "It's clear your family doesn't do anything like the rest of us. If telekinesis kicked in, there's always the possibility something else may have. Then again, Max only has his animal communication and telekinesis. A lot of us don't have a wide variety of natural abilities. I didn't even think it was possible until Brandy came along."

Ryan asked for more detail on when his telekinesis had kicked in, and he shook his head. "Yeah, while I understand her mom's concern and keeping things quiet, her words definitely struck a protective chord with you. Max and Ethan had both tapped into their power the same way."

"Well, I'd like the quick, quick version of handling it because Daphyne's working with Vanessa now so she can confront Olsabir," he stated, his body humming with nerves at the mere thought of her doing it.

"What?" Serena snapped as Ethan said, "That makes a lot more sense now."

"Huh?" Brandy said.

Ethan scooted forward to the edge of the couch. "Well, I had a vision of Vanessa in front of this white-haired man in a charcoal-gray power suit. It has to be the same guy you're talking about because his teeth elongated into sharp points and his eyes flashed black."

Carter lowered his tea to his knee. "When the hell did you have that vision? Were you not going to tell me?"

"Calm down. I only had it on the way here in the car." Ethan shook his head and sighed. "I wasn't this bad when Aja was screwing with us, was I?"

Brandy giggled. "You were. I think we all were."

"Blame our mate bonds. It makes us overreact," Ryan stated.

Brandy's giggle turned into a roar of laughter. "You think?" She pointed her thumb toward Ryan. "This one here tried castrating Peter, his own best friend."

chapter 33

"How'd it go?"

Vanessa ran a hand over Carter's cheek and smiled before turning to grab her seatbelt. "I'm exhausted. Why didn't you tell me using magic wipes you?"

Once the seatbelt clicked into place, she felt Carter release the brake. "I don't usually overuse it, and it's been a very long time since I started. I get what you mean though because after working with the family today, I'm beat."

"How about you feed me something juicy, and we can play show-and-tell?"

"That's funny because I'd love to play show-and-tell with something juicy—oof."

Vanessa shook her head at Carter as he rubbed his belly. "As much as I want to play hide the sausage with you, we both know I was referring to our magic, naughty man."

He cast her a sheepish grin. "I can't help it, sweetheart. I've missed you, and burying myself in you after this long-ass day is all I can think about."

Vanessa laid her hand on his thigh and ran it up to the zipper. "How about this? You take a scenic route to food, and I mean some fried chicken with mashed potatoes and coleslaw, and I'll give you a little treat to hold you over until later?"

She smirked at his groan of approval.

"*Fuck,* I like that a lot..."

The words had come out of her mouth without a thought. She had never given anyone road head before. Looking around the car nervously, she chewed on her lower lip as she questioned her offer.

"No one will see you," he said, cupping her neck.

"Okay, don't kill us though."

Vanessa tugged on the pull tab of his zipper, her mouth watering when his erection sprung forth. The man was not a fan of underwear it seemed. Carter took himself in hand and pumped up and down the shaft as she released her seatbelt before shifting for better access.

"Damn, I wish I could finger you right now. When we get home, I want you riding my face, hear me?"

His words made her sex clench and flood with desire. "I hear you." She moaned and squeezed her thighs together.

She lowered her face and wrapped her lips around his engorged tip. Carter let loose a string of expletives as one hand rubbed her back in soothing circles. A little niggling fear of them crashing had her determined to make him climax in record time. Using her mouth, tongue, and hand, she aimed to give him a blow job he would never forget.

He thrusted his hips, and his dick slammed into the back of her throat. Thankful her gag reflex had not kicked in, she concentrated on breathing through her nose and tapped into her magic. She sent a teasing breeze over his balls and smiled around a mouthful of dick at his hiss of pleasure.

Within seconds, Carter gripped her hair tightly. Unintelligible words escaped his lips, and his body tightened under her.

"Fuck, fuck, fuck, ah…"

Vanessa swallowed and licked before giving him a sweet smile. "Feel better, baby?"

He peered from the road to her with labored breaths. "I… uh—"

She giggled as his hands readjusted on the steering wheel, and she clicked her seatbelt in place once again. "Now remember, you promised me lots of food."

"Food? Woman's talking about food after my brain nearly exploded from that blow job," he muttered and shook his head.

She giggled. "Well, your brain kinda did explode, all in my mouth."

His mouth opened and closed before one hand tucked himself back into his jeans. "I'm starting to think you're a siren and not a nymph—no, never mind. Definitely a nymph—nymphomaniac."

She raised a brow. "Sounds like you're complaining."

Carter shook his head quickly. "Oh, hell no, that's not a complaint. I'd happily die in your arms because of your insatiable needs."

Carter kept his part of the bargain and not only managed to get them to dinner but fed her a crazy amount of food. The drive back to his place was less adventurous than the one toward food.

Vanessa debated taking a nap before sharing what she had learned as she kicked off her shoes, but Carter tossed her over his shoulder. "Oh God, don't make me puke!" Without a word, he set her on her feet, then scooped her into his arms.

"Carter?" she asked, partly amused and partly aroused when he stripped off her shirt as soon as they reached his bedroom.

He shook his head. "No talky-talk. I'm ready for my dessert, and I've been a good boy."

Hell if he wasn't a good boy.

Carter buried his face between her legs in no time. He expertly drew out her orgasm with his mouth and fingers before pushing her onto her hands and knees. The sex was not graceful or slow. It was raw and claiming.

There would be bruises on her hips from the grip he had on them, but she loved every minute of it.

Vanessa cleared her throat, her chest rising and falling quickly. "Nap now, show-and-tell later."

Carter pulled her against his side and brushed off the hair sticking to her sweaty face. He offered no words, only a soft kiss to her forehead. Her sex throbbed in a delicious way as she faded, wrapped in the arms of the man she loved.

chapter 34

The smell of flowers and damp moss filled his lungs, drawing him from sleep. His dream-induced fog began to clear at the sound of running water. Carter turned on his side, searching for Vanessa, but only found cool sheets where her body had lain.

He pushed out his magic and sensed her nearby as he struggled to wake. Between the use of magic in his lesson and losing himself in Vanessa's body, he was spent. He could roll over and easily sleep for another twelve hours.

Instead, he cracked his lids open again in search of his mate. For a moment, he questioned where he was. Vines covered his walls, flowers blossomed before his eyes throughout his room, and a bubbling could be heard from behind him. It reminded him of the brook through the portal.

Vanessa sat ramrod straight at the end of his bed wearing one of his T-shirts. Her hair was a mess from their lovemaking, and his chest filled with pride to call her his.

Carter pushed up onto an elbow. "What's going on, sweetheart?"

She visibly startled and peered over her shoulder. "You scared me!"

He sat up and moved closer, giving her a kiss on the shoulder. "Sorry. Did you do all this?" he asked, waving a hand before them.

She graced him with a beaming smile. "Mhmm... Mom taught me nymphs are linked with the earth. It's getting easier each time I call forth different plants or water. Water is the easiest for us, and Mom said it was because we were naiads, like Mia assumed."

He grinned at her excitement. "How do you feel? It's not too taxing, is it?"

She shook her head. "Yesterday was rough, but now? This is invigorating! I feel both powerful and in awe over what I can do. It's the craziest thing."

"Yesterday?" he asked, searching for his clock.

"Oh, sorry!" Vanessa waved her hand, and the vines over his nightstand moved like a curtain.

Five in the morning.

Carter stood from the bed. "How long have you been up, sweetheart?"

Vanessa's gaze moved down his naked body. "Not sure. I think an hour or two. I woke up feeling really energized."

Carter padded to the bathroom and relieved himself before leaning against the doorframe. "So, tonight is our family dinner…"

Her eyes moved down to his semi-erect dick. "You have no shame," she muttered before attempting to complete his sentence. "But?"

He shrugged. "Maybe I'm hoping the more you see it, the more you'll take advantage of me."

"But what?" she asked, ignoring him.

"But, some of the others think if you're ready for it, you should show your force to Olsabir tonight," he said, not really on board with the suggestion but ready to move on with their lives. "I mean, we would all go, but it's up to you if you want to try today. If not, I'll ask Joel to join you again at the shop until you're ready."

Vanessa's mouth opened and closed a few times. "I, um… Well, my mom said she'd stand at my side when the time came. She suggested a few simple things to do to put the status of me being a human to rest."

Carter knelt next to her. "The most important question is, do you feel ready? You've only tapped into your magic less than twenty-four hours ago."

"What do you think?" she whispered.

He shook his head. "What I think doesn't really matter. My instinct is to whisk you away and protect you under spells so no one will come after you again. Whether you decide today is the day or a month from now, we'll stand at your side. Oh, and before I forget, you need to close the shop on the twenty-second."

Her brows pinched. "What's on the twenty-second?"

"You'll be my plus one to Serena and Ethan's wedding."

Her lips parted in surprise. "Seriously? How did I not know this? That's in *two* weeks! What the hell am I going to get them?"

Carter chuckled. "I've been meaning to mention it, and well, other things have come up." He looked around his room and grinned. "You could always provide the flowers," he said with a wink.

She shook her head. "I'm sure that's covered by now." Vanessa dropped her head in her hands and sighed. "What the hell should I do?"

"A gift certificate to—"

"No." Vanessa chuckled and met his eyes. "Not about the wedding gift, about me and the stupid demon who has it out for me."

"What does your gut tell you?"

Vanessa looked around the room and waved a hand around. "*This* was rather easy. My body is vibrating with all this added energy, and it's begging me to connect. I don't even remember what I felt like before I tapped into this. Going up against a demon, something I didn't even believe existed until a few months ago? I-I don't know!"

Carter finished pulling on some shorts and sat next to her, then pulled her onto his lap. Her arms wrapped around his neck, and they held each other for a moment, giving and receiving comfort. He breathed her in and noticed her scent had changed some. It was more earthy and flowery but not from a bottle.

When he pulled back, their gazes met. "It's okay not to know. No one is forcing you to do this today. Why don't I make us some breakfast and we can relax, remember what it was like before you learned all of this?"

She scoffed, her lips twitching. "I'm not sure I can forget all of this now that I know it."

"Not asking you to. Let's just set it aside and see if an answer comes to us while we're *not* thinking on it." Carter slid an arm under her knees and pushed to his feet.

Her answering giggle made him smile. She laid her head against his chest, trusting him to carry her without any doubts, and his heart filled with so much love, he wondered if it would burst.

Carter made them scrambled eggs and toast after setting her on the countertop near him. He pegged her with questions about the boutique to keep her wandering thoughts from returning to the elephant in the room.

They laughed, smiled, and kissed, like any other normal couple. He knew there was still much to learn about her, and he was eager to do it.

"Go find something for us to watch. I'll be done in a second," he told her as he made quick work of cleaning the small mess they had made.

She grabbed his bicep as she rolled to her toes and kissed his cheek. "Thank you."

Carter paused in the middle of rinsing the pan to watch her hips sway under his T-shirt. Her bare legs teased him with each step.

"Focus, baby," she teased, watching him over her shoulder.

Carter laughed. "Busted!"

A few minutes later, Carter dried his hands on a towel and tossed it onto the counter. Vanessa had become engrossed with a reality cooking show in the time it had taken him to finish. He shifted Vanessa so her back was to his chest as they lay along the couch. She sighed as she relaxed against him and linked their fingers over her belly.

He was unsure how much time had passed when banging on the front door startled them both. The furniture around them levitated, and vines sprouted over the cushions. His brows raised, and a gasp slipped from her lips.

"You expecting someone?" she whispered.

Carter shook his head as he drew in a breath. One by one, the furniture returned to the ground. "It's still pretty early for visitors," he told her, noticing the clock on the cable box read 7:33 a.m.

Bang. Bang. Bang.

"I can hear you two. Open the damn door!"

Vanessa's chin dropped to her chest as she chuckled. "Of course it's Georgia, because she's probably the only person in this world who doesn't care about visiting hours."

"I heard that!"

Carter put a hand on her thigh, stopping her from standing. "I'll get it."

He opened the door and watched the annoyed werewolf's face transform, and her tongue ran along her lips. Carter's brows raised in amusement. "I hope you didn't wake any neighbors."

Georgia inspected his shirtless state and shook her head. "Do you answer the door for all your guests this way?" she asked as she stepped past him.

He shrugged. "I'm not dressed for visitors."

When Georgia stopped in her steps, he looked past her at a pissed-off Vanessa. Flowers decorated her hair, vines had wrapped around her body in a way that made his dick twitch, and his living room was suddenly the outdoors.

Georgia gasped. "It's true."

"Sweetheart, everything okay?" he asked, padding closer but aware of the hard glint in her eyes.

Vanessa focused on Georgia. "You realize he's mine, right?" she asked firmly, and vines inched their way toward their visitor.

Georgia cocked her head. "Carter? Yeah, babe. He's all yours, but he can't go answering doors like that and not expect me to stare."

Vanessa snarled, and he felt a sudden push of magic from her.

Carter cleared his throat. "Sweetheart?" he said soothingly, waiting for her to look at him. "I'm going to go change while you two catch up."

"Good idea," she hissed, and her nostrils flared.

He rushed toward the bedroom, smiling like an idiot. The woman had just shown her possessive side, and his dick approved.

chapter 35

"Girl, you realize he's all yours, right?"

Blood rushed through her ears, making the words muffled but loud enough she could make them out. A strange sensation coursed through her as her body vibrated with the desire to string Georgia up by the ankles.

A growl vibrated through the room. "Vanessa!"

She met Georgia's eyes, noting they glowed yellow, nearly a golden color. A part of Vanessa knew this was her best friend who would never hurt her. The other part of her demanded she pay for the way she had drunk Carter in.

When he returned to the room, they had not made any progress. Well, that was not true. The arches to the room were decorated with beautiful vines and wildflowers.

Carter's chest blocked Georgia, obstructing Vanessa's view in the standoff. He grabbed her face and crushed his mouth to hers. Love, desire, and truth poured into her. She reached out and grabbed onto the polo he'd changed into, her body swaying with the force of his kiss.

The tension in her body lessened, and he pressed his forehead to hers. "I belong to you."

Any lingering anger and jealousy melted from her. "Shit…" She rolled her eyes at the arrogant smirk tipping his lips. "Shut up." She groaned and stepped around him. "Georgia?"

"I'm not sure, are you going to attack me with more jungle?"

"Sorry."

Georgia shook her head. "Girl, you know I'd never go after what was yours, not that I ever could with this one. Carter has eyes only for you. I was simply admiring the view."

Vanessa's shoulders slumped. "I *know!* Something just came over me…"

"Damn soul mates. Nuh uh, I don't want anything to do with that shit," Georgia said, offering Vanessa a hug.

She wrapped her arms around her best friend and soaked in the comfort. "Seriously, I'm so sorry. I couldn't snap out of it."

Georgia stepped back. "Clearly."

Carter wrapped an arm around her waist, claiming her once she was clear of Georgia. "So, would you like to tell us what warranted such an early visit? I'm sure it had nothing to do with me or watching Vanessa lose control."

"Yeah, what's going on?" Vanessa asked.

Georgia moved around them and dropped into the chair next to the couch. "Peter had me on a run—we're struggling to find the other Sivella compound—and as soon as I got back, he gave me an update. So the person after you is a demon?"

"Yeah."

Georgia nodded. "And you're not going to address the fact that since I saw you last, you're clearly no longer a human?"

Vanessa opened her mouth and closed it before laughing. "So much has happened since we last talked."

"Clearly. So, how'd you tap into your nymph side?"

Her eyes rounded and then narrowed. "How the hell did you know?"

Georgia tapped her nose. "Nymphs are rare. Other than your mom, I've only come across two others, now three with you."

"You knew?" Vanessa whispered. She wanted to be pissed it had been kept from her. Not only her mother but her best friend had kept the information to themselves.

Carter guided her to the couch. "Sweetheart, no one wanted to keep secrets from you."

She looked at him through blurry eyes, tears threatening to fall. "I get it, but it doesn't stop it from hurting."

Georgia slipped to the floor and took her hand. "No more secrets, I promise. That was the last thing. It wasn't my place to say anything about your mom, and you just never showed any signs."

Vanessa nodded, unable to speak through the lump in her throat.

"When we bonded, we must have awakened her half-nymph side," Carter said before recounting the incident with the lycan. "It was through him we learned Olsabir is who has his hairs on her."

"Olsabir?" Georgia asked, a brow raised. "That guy's a joke. Volark was the real deal. This guy's a wannabe."

Vanessa tilted her head. "Mom said something like that. What do you know about him?"

"His biggest threat is the people he surrounds himself with. He has a group of tubars who follow him, and a couple lycans. I wouldn't be surprised if some of the packless werewolves do work for hire with him. He's just trying to look badass, but a strong enough witch would eliminate him from the board easily enough."

"Mom suggested I confront him. She said if he saw I wasn't a human threatening to expose the supernaturals, he'd back off."

Georgia shrugged. "You could. Or we could just get rid of him and his cronies. We really don't need any more kids falling into the drugs and scams they run… Say," Georgia said and pushed to her feet. "I'd bet my right tit the person who broke into your store was one of those humans. You mentioned a lycan attack as well. Any others?"

Carter squeezed her waist. "A tubar was lurking around, and Xander got rid of him."

Georgia clapped excitedly. "See, he started from the bottom and worked his way up. I bet he'll be the next one to show. If his men couldn't get to you, he'll do it himself so he doesn't look like a pussy in front of them."

Vanessa turned toward Carter and held his eyes, adrenaline pumping through her. "What should we do?"

Georgia waved her hands in the air. "Duh, let's take this asshole out so you two can get your happily ever after!"

Carter shrugged. "What does your gut tell you?"

It was not the first time he had asked that question. Earlier, she had felt so much anxiety and turmoil, she could not tune into her bladder, let alone her instincts. Her head bobbed without thought. "I'm tired of living in fear. If he's going to come after me, I'd rather get to him first."

He grinned. "And I'll be at your side. Let me call up Brandy." Carter pushed to his feet. "Georgia, can I assume you're in too?"

"Hell yeah, I am. No way am I not protecting this family."

The air around Vanessa became impossibly still. Carter stopped and turned to stare, his face mirroring hers. Blood rushed through her ears, and a lump the size of Texas lodged in her throat.

Carter cleared his throat first. "What are you talking about?"

Georgia tapped her nose and nodded toward Vanessa. "This one is fertile myrtle right now, and it's clear you two have been going at it like a pair of bunnies. Unless of course you've been wrapping your tool?"

Her words replayed in Vanessa's head. Could she be pregnant? They had used condoms after the first two times, but they were not foolproof. She and Carter hadn't been together long. Was she ready to be a mom?

chapter 36

Carter stared into the distance as Georgia's words settled. Images of Vanessa round with his child sent a flurry of excitement to his heart.

"Nessie? Are you okay?" Georgia asked, drawing his attention back to his mate—in the now and not the future.

He looked toward her and found her white as a ghost. "Vanessa?"

"Am I pregnant?" she whispered, hope and fear flashing in her eyes.

Georgia grabbed a hand and breathed in deeply. She smiled at Vanessa. "No, honey. If you want to be though, we better get this demon out of your life so you two can get to business."

Vanessa exhaled a harsh breath and met his eyes.

"I don't know," she said.

Carter smiled. *"I'm on board for whatever you want, sweetheart. Remember this, we're in no rush, and I'm not going anywhere."*

His cell vibrated in his hand. "It's Ethan," he announced.

"Hey, E, what's going on?"

"We found where Olsabir camps out," he stated.

Carter shook his head and chuckled. "You know, I find myself less creeped out when you do this."

"Do what—oh, yeah, sorry about that."

He closed his eyes and shook his head. "No, you're not. I'm just glad it's you who got that power and not Junior. He's pretty unbearable now. I couldn't imagine him if he could legit check up on us whenever."

Ethan's chuckle sounded through the phone. "No shit!" The phone became muffled as he suspected his brother spoke to someone else. "Sorry about that... Brandy says Peter and Joel are also in."

Carter spoke to Ethan long enough to get the address of where Olsabir was and where they would meet. When he turned to face the women, he frowned at their hushed whispers. "Ladies?"

Vanessa's gaze barely met his before dropping to her lap. "I don't want you going..."

"Excuse me?" he asked, looking from her to Georgia and back.

She sucked in her lower lip and stared at her friend. Georgia shook her head in reply, "Nuh-uh, Nessie, keep me out of this. I'm going to the ladies' room while you two figure this out."

Carter took the spot Georgia had vacated and pulled one of Vanessa's hands into both of his. "Talk to me."

Her sigh tore at his heart. "Baby, I just can't handle it if something happens to you."

Carter smiled and lifted her hand to his lips. "I feel the same way, and as much as I want to lock you up in my room and go handle this, I know I can't. You don't have a chance in hell facing Olsabir without me at your side—not because I don't think you can't handle him but because I refuse to let you go without me at your side where I belong."

Her lips pulled into a thin line before pursing. "I suppose I wouldn't let you go without me either."

Carter chuckled. "I don't suppose you would."

"All right, now that that's all settled, can we go figure out where this asswipe is?" Georgia asked, leaning against the wall leading to the bathroom.

Carter ignored her a moment longer and claimed Vanessa's lips. "No need," he said, staring into Vanessa's eyes. "The others called to tell me they found Olsabir and where we need to meet them."

"Damn, you Brodericks really don't play around."

"Not when it comes to our mates we don't," Carter answered and pulled Vanessa to her feet.

They piled into Carter's Audi and headed for the rendezvous point. His brows raised when he spotted the rather large gathering in the ominous parking lot. Max, Ethan, Brandy, and their mates stood in a circle alongside Peter and Joel.

"Well shit, I'm not sure why I bothered coming along," Georgia said, peering through the windshield from between the front two seats.

"You love me. That's why," Vanessa said, reaching back and wrapping her arm around the werewolf's neck.

"About time!" Brandy called as they reached the group.

"What's the plan?" Georgia called to Peter.

Peter pointed with his thumb behind him. "There's a few mindless humans hanging out, and Ethan is going to help them forget Olsabir."

Carter's brows raised to his hairline. "You can erase people's memories now?"

"Serena knows a spell that will help me scrub all things supernatural from their minds," Ethan said with a shrug.

"It will be the most effective coming from him," Serena said.

Peter pointed at Carter. "You, your brothers, Joel, and I will clear out the tubars, lycans, and werewolves so the ladies can back up Vanessa."

Carter nodded, partially hating the idea of not being at her side but understanding his part in the plan. "I don't like it, but I get it."

Georgia placed a hand on Carter's shoulder. "I'll keep her safe."

"We'll all keep her safe," Brandy replied as Serena said, "You know we won't let anything bad happen to her."

"How about nothing happen to all of you?" Max stated, his arm wrapped firmly around Claudia's waist.

Claudia turned in Max's arms. "We survived Benito's compound, and everything on this guy says he's more of a talker than a fighter."

"Can we get this started before I either piss my pants or change my mind?" Vanessa asked.

Brandy gasped. "Whoa."

Carter peered down and noted vines were wrapped around Vanessa's arms, and an ethereal glow was emanating from her. "I think she's ready to go." He chuckled and kissed her temple.

The others said quick good-byes to their mates and headed in to take out the first round of Olsabir's followers. Ethan cleared the humans hanging around, but Carter did not get to do much with the swift work of Ryan, Peter, and Joel.

He pulled the knife he had been given from the demon in front of him a second before it burst into flames. Carter moved the knife from one hand to the other and stretched his fingers. "I never would have guessed stabbing someone worked so many muscles."

Ryan laughed and slapped Carter's shoulder. "That's why I use my magic whenever I can."

"I keep forgetting I can tap into it."

Max saddled up to them. "There are at least two other animals around here, werewolves from what I can tell."

Peter lifted his nose in the air and emitted a low bark.

"Peter says one of them is a rat, but he smells them," Max said.

"Serena said they came across a lycan but no others. We should probably head their way in case there are any they missed," Ethan said.

"Wouldn't you know if there were others?" Carter asked as they made their way down a hall.

Ethan rubbed his temple. "Usually I would, but until the threat's gone, I don't trust anything. I don't like that they are facing them solo."

chapter 37

A wreath of flowers decorated her head as they moved down a long hall. Vanessa's heartbeat thrummed at her neck. Her pulse was strong and steady, reminding her she was alive and how much was at stake if they did not accomplish the removal of Olsabir.

Georgia and Claudia growled at her back, and the others paused. Magic filled the space around them as a young man stepped from a room. His eyes crinkled on the edges as he stared right at them, only he did not see them.

"Human," Serena whispered and tapped her temple with two fingers.

Vanessa watched his eyes go blank before he shook his head and glanced around.

"Where the hell am I?" he muttered.

Another wave of magic flowed from Serena, and Vanessa watched his eyes fill with an *aha* moment.

"I should turn myself in."

They stepped out of the way when he moved toward them, never seeing the two witches, werewolves, and nymph past the barrier hiding them.

"What's he turning himself in for?" Brandy asked.

Serena shrugged. "Ethan tuned in and said he saw a jewelry shop, so my best guess is he's responsible for the damage at your shop."

Brandy wrapped her fingers around Vanessa's upper arm when vines unfurled. "Whoa, girl. Remember, he was just working for Olsabir. He's the real reason we're here."

Vanessa sucked in a deep breath, and the vines wrapped her in a caress. "You're right."

The hall became musty the farther they walked, and the smell of rotting flesh filled her nose. Each of them shared a look as Claudia and Georgia growled deep in their throats. The sound was menacing, and she was thankful to be on the beautiful wolves' side.

"What's wrong?" Carter asked.

"I think we're close," she said and closed her eyes a moment.

Digging deeply like her mother had shown her, she prepared to face the demon she sensed in the next room. "Do you think he knows?" she whispered when her gaze landed on the metal door.

"Maybe? I know Volark did, but he also kidnapped Ryan to draw me in." Brandy cleared her throat. "Ready, ladies?" she asked a moment later when they circled the door.

"No, but I'm ready for this shit to be done." Vanessa dropped her hands to her sides and shook them before readying herself by pointing her palms toward the door.

Serena chuckled. "Fair enough. Brandy?"

The door hinges flared a hot red before the weight of the door bent them, and Brandy sent it flying into the room.

"What the... Who's there?" a man demanded, his voice thick and dark.

Vanessa sucked a deep breath into her lungs and stepped forward. She felt them at her back and knew they would keep her safe. Without a thought, vines ripped from the ground and pulled him to his knees. "I'm here, Olsabir. I heard you were looking for me, so we thought an introduction was necessary."

Olsabir met her eyes. White hair capped his head, and his black pits for eyes stared at her from his oval-shaped face. He wore an impeccable gray suit as he raised his chin in her direction. The man—no, demon—reminded her of any of the hundreds of politicians she had seen.

"And who exactly are you?" he asked, as elongated teeth took the place of the pristine white ones that had been there only moments before.

A vine crawled up his leg, to his arm, and finally wrapped around his neck. "Vanessa Rayne, the woman you've sent tubars, humans, and lycans after."

His brows pinched together. "No, there must be some sort of misunderstanding because the Vanessa Rayne I was after was a *human*," he said, spitting out the latter as if it left a bad taste in his mouth. "And it's clear you are *not*."

Georgia snapped her teeth at him, spittle dripping from her mouth.

Vanessa chuckled. "Maybe if you'd done your homework, things would be clearer."

She heard a noise at her back and stiffened, the vine tightening around Olsabir.

"It's just us," Carter said.

Her heart stuttered and she sucked in a breath, focusing on the bastard before her.

"You have a lot of friends," Olsabir said, his gaze roving the room. She felt him push against her hold and stand to his feet. He peered down, a sickening smile touching his lips. "Hmm..."

Vanessa did not know what he did exactly to warn her. Perhaps it was the slight shift of his right shoulder or maybe the sudden stillness which overtook him, but when he attacked, she pulled back on the vine wrapped around his neck. His eyes rounded with surprise, and a smirk tipped her mouth upward.

"What should we do?" she asked the group at her side.

Metal glinted from her left. "Drive this through his heart, and he'll stop being a problem," Serena announced.

"If we let him live, he's only going to continue being a problem, not for us but others," Ryan stated from Brandy's side.

"One of us can do it if you don't want—"

"No," Vanessa snapped, interrupting Brandy. She put out her hand toward Serena and accepted the cold metal. The dagger's handle was heavy and intricately woven with a beautiful design. "I got this."

A hand on her shoulder stopped her. She turned at the familiar weight and met Carter's eyes. Neither spoke, sharing only a look that spoke volumes. For a moment she worried he would kiss her, diminishing her position before the demon, but he only nodded and dropped his hand.

Power surged through her at his support, and she raised her chin before turning on her heels. Vanessa pulled the vines tightly, securing Olsabir in place as she took a few steps toward him.

She debated asking him for his last words but decided quickly they were of no consequence to any of them. "Should've done your homework," she whispered and sent the knife into his heart via a gust of wind.

Surprise barely registered on his face before he burst into flames like the other demons she had seen her friends kill. The vines that had held him lay limp before she absorbed them back within her.

Vanessa still did not understand how she could call them, but she knew they were as much a part of her as the hair growing from her head.

"Nice job, girl!" Georgia said and clapped her hands as she stood completely naked before her.

No one seemed to react to her nude state, but Vanessa could not help but find a spot on the wall to focus on. She thought maybe with time she could adjust, but when she found Claudia in a similar state, Vanessa realized she was far less evolved than the others.

"I'm glad to see you didn't draw that out," Peter called from behind her, giving her a reason to turn.

Carter pulled her into his arms and crushed her mouth with his. The kiss was deep and full of emotion. His tongue met hers, tangling and dancing in the only body-tingling way it knew. The world around them fell away. The fact she just killed Olsabir became a distant memory as her thoughts became consumed by Carter.

Her thighs clenched together, and her nipples tightened into hard peaks as desire flooded her. Vanessa jumped into his arms, their sexes lining as she became consumed by the need to be filled.

"Whoa," someone called.

Carter gripped her ass so hard, she briefly wondered if he'd leave bruises. His forehead came to hers, their short breaths teasing each other's lips.

"How about you two wait until you get home to fuck each other's brains?" Peter called as he slipped into his jeans.

"Eww," Brandy cried. "I don't need any more of a visual.

"Babycakes, you and Ryan were worse than them." Peter chuckled and tossed his arm over her shoulders, then walked her out of the room.

Carter slid her down his front and kissed her forehead. "God, I love you so much," he whispered when their eyes met.

Tears sprung to her eyes, making his handsome face blur. "I love you too!"

He caressed her cheeks. "Why are you crying then?"

She giggled as she shrugged. "I don't know. Maybe because you make me happy and I don't have to worry about—" Vanessa turned to where Olsabir's ashes had been. "Where'd it go?"

"Brandy cleared them, but you two were too busy sucking faces," Georgia said, tugging the hem of her shirt to her hips.

Vanessa narrowed her eyes. "Where did you get clothes from?"

"Max. He conjured mine, Peter's, and Claudia's so we didn't have to walk out of here in our birthday suits. Handy little trick the witches have figured out."

Carter chuckled. "It's next on my list of things to learn." He slung an arm over each of their shoulders. "Why don't we get the hell out of here so I can take my woman home?"

"If it means no one else has to be witness to you freaks, I'm down," Georgia replied.

Vanessa peered across Carter as he guided them back out. "Thanks again for being here."

"Nessie, I'll always have your back. Gotta say though, I'm really relieved knowing you can protect yourself now."

Carter kissed Vanessa's hair and released them both when they reached a door at the end of the hall. "I'm with Georgia on that."

Vanessa chuckled. "Make that three."

They reached the large group gathered around, and she noticed Joel. "Hey, where'd you go?"

"Peter told me to keep an eye on the outside in case any surprises showed," he said, stepping forward to hug her. "I heard you handled yourself well."

Vanessa pulled back and smiled. "Not too shabby, if I do say so myself."

"Well, here's hoping the rest of you can keep your asses out of trouble," Peter announced, a single brow raised as he took each of them in.

Brandy giggled. "Edward is the only one of us who hasn't fallen on his face. Only time will tell us."

"Is he bringing anyone to the wedding?" Serena asked as she placed a hand on her hip. "Getting him to agree he'd stay in town for it was like pulling teeth."

Carter scoffed. "Edward's always brooding and alone. I'm honestly surprised each time he makes it to a family dinner."

"Speaking of which, we should probably head over to James's. I bet Andrea still cooked for an army even though we weren't sure if we'd be done in time." Brandy looked at Joel and Georgia. "You two are joining us, right?"

"I—" they said in unison.

"If I'm part of this family…" She looked at Carter for confirmation before continuing. "Then so are they."

Ryan chuckled. "She definitely belongs in this family."

chapter 38

The last thing Carter wanted to do was surround himself with family. He was eager to take Vanessa to bed and show her over and over again how much he loved her. Of course, he also knew there was no backing out of family dinner.

They made their appearance and ate delicious food, and once everyone had a chance to praise Vanessa for doing so well against Olsabir, he whisked her away. Thankfully, Peter had offered to drive Georgia to the house for her car.

As soon as the door shut behind them, he started ripping off their clothes. Carter took her against a wall in the foyer, on the couch, and atop the kitchen island. He drew out each orgasm, enjoying every pulse, scream, and declaration of love they shared.

Somehow, they made it into the shower for their last round of lovemaking. He would never forget the way she looked on her knees with her lips wrapped around his dick and her eyes wide and sparkling.

On shaky legs, they cleaned themselves before he managed one last burst of energy and carried her to bed. His heart had finally stopped racing, and his lungs found their natural rhythm.

Carter ran a hand over her hip as she curled into his side. "Car?" she muttered, her breath tickling his chest.

"Hmm?"

"Am I really safe?"

With his free hand, he tilted her chin until their eyes locked. "As far as I'm concerned you are. I'd die before any harm ever came to a single hair on your body."

She shook her head. "Nothing would ever touch either of us so long as we have each other."

He grinned. "You belong to me, and I to you. My love for you is never ending."

"I love you," she declared and brushed a kiss on his mouth.

"I'm so glad I was at the hospital when you brought Tyler in."

"Me too, I just wish we could have kept him safe," she whispered as her eyes misted.

His heart clenched at her guilt. "It wasn't your fault. Peter told me Tyler had got in with some people he shouldn't have. His death had nothing to do with Olsabir looking for you."

Relief flashed in her eyes before she laid her cheek on his chest. He ran his fingers through her hair as she gave in to exhaustion.

He realized then he was in heaven.

There was no other explanation for it. The peace he felt with her tucked into his limp and satiated body was indescribable. Vanessa, whom he would do absolutely anything for and had the biggest heart, was his mate, his partner, his everything.

cursed Cuck

Coming 2021

Edward Broderick was anything but lucky.

His intuition made him suave in both business and life. Unfortunately, his debonair style went out the window when an ethereal beauty slipped into his life. No woman had made him feel like a tongue-tied fifteen-year-old before.

Free-spirited Mia Hemlock didn't live by others' expectations. Yet her easy life was shaken by the arrogant and awkward, yet handsome, man. Not even her earth magic could ground her heart when she became consumed by the man.

Will they accept the goddess's love match, or will they allow misunderstandings and greed to force them apart?

about the author

AJ Renee grew up in a military family and moved around until her family settled in Florida. She graduated from the University of Central Florida with a M.S. in Criminal Justice and a B.S. in Psychology. She currently resides in Virginia and spends her time with her Air Force husband, three young daughters, and cat. She loves to travel and see family and friends whenever she gets a chance. She has a love of music, movies, and anything that can make her laugh. AJ believes in reading books with humor and mystery that end in a happily ever after to help ease our minds and hearts of life's daily struggles.

To stay up to date on new releases, go to www.AJRenee.com.

also by aj renee

ST. FLEUR SERIES:

Widower's Aura

Always Mine

Duplicity

No Going Back

Taxed by Love

Complications

LOVE IN SCRUBS SERIES:

Joshua

Jason

Wes

BRODERICK COVEN SERIES:

Cursed Love

Cursed Sight

Cursed Whispers

Cursed Touch

Cursed Luck ~ *Coming 2021*

OTHER TITLES:

Finding Love at the Falls... (Short Story)

Fractured Fairytales Book One

Beauty Unmasked

Winter's Surprise

A Deadly World: Vampires in Paris

Billionaires Club

Unlucky in Love

Take Two: A Collection of Second Chance Stories

Made in the USA
Middletown, DE
01 August 2021